They Didn't See the Flowers

Kristin Kraus

ELOQUENT
BEE PRESS

This novella's story is fictitious. Certain long-standing institutions, agencies, and public offices that are mentioned exist, but most of the characters involved are wholly imaginary with the exception of some real historical people. The events of Africville, however, were real.

Cover design by Max Yenin (Yenin.art Studio)

Cataloguing data available from Library and Archives Canada

ISBN: 978-0-9808896-4-2

About the Author

Kristin Kraus is an author and teacher currently living in British Columbia, Canada. Her first book is a collection of short stories for adults titled *Monkey Sandwich Stories*, her two novellas are *The Oyster Garden*, and *Hell If I Know: Polaroids and Prison Riots*. One of the most enjoyable aspects of writing for Kristin is collecting details about places and interactions acquired through travelling and observing. Kristin has always enjoyed reading and writing and remains fascinated by what people do and say.

Acknowledgements

Any published work requires the collaboration of others. No author is an island. For the production of this novella, I thank Amie Roussel for her photography work on the back cover, Jane Usher and Kellie Jardine for their editing skills which helped me to improve my writing greatly, and Maksym Yenin of Yenin.art Studio for his excellent work on my cover and logos.

Family and friends have been very supportive of my writing over the years, so I thank them as well, especially my husband.

I'd like to give a shout-out to the beautiful province of Nova Scotia for inspiring this story. I visited there with my family in the summer of 2013 and was struck by the rich history of the area.

This novella is dedicated to the people who lived in Africville and their descendants and to all Indigenous people.

"I did not see the flowers."

—Gus Wedderburn, councillor in Halifax, NS who ordered the relocation of the residents of Africville, when later shown a photo of the village

Contents

Prologue

This is the story of people in Nova Scotia, the tale of their hopes, dreams, and failures, a microcosm of humanity in all its glory and sadness, successes and near-misses. The generations described here are not so different from those past and present in their struggle to find meaning in this country with so many months of the year spent shrouded in ice and snow. I invite you to reflect on your own place here, in Canada, in whatever city or town you may live, where Voltaire saw only "quelques arpents de neige" (acres of snow).

2023

Chapter One

Mid-December

Back in a bed at the geriatric wing of the hospital for the second time in less than a month, David Kennedy found himself thinking about how this little neck of the woods where he'd been born and raised has been a real hotbed of historical crises. Name another part of Canada that has had an explosion as damaging as the Halifax detonation of 1917. David remembered how the famous Nova Scotian author Hugh MacLennan even wrote about it in his novel *Barometer Rising*, and his son told him that a band called the Tragically Hip wrote a song honouring MacLennan called "Courage." As if the deadly detonation of picric acid, TNT, and gun cotton wasn't enough for Halifax during the Great War, yet another blast, known as the Bedford Magazine Explosion, rocked the same area in 1945. Bedford, north of Halifax, was where David Kennedy was just five years old when a barge in the harbour exploded at 6:30 p.m., spreading flames to the dock where ammunition awaited. As an adult, he'd read about how a terrifying chain reaction of fires and blasts shattered windows, crumpled roofs, and cracked buildings. Fortunately, not many injuries resulted this second time as the city had evacuation plans in place after the 1917 fiasco, but one person who did get hurt was David's father. His mama said her poor husband was never right in the head after that bad concussion, and the family had to rely more on her domestic jobs in the homes of wealthy white people.

According to records, Black people in the North area of Halifax that became known as Africville originally consisted of Maroons from Jamaica escaping slavery from the British and refugees from the War of 1812 from the Chesapeake Bay Area of the USA. Far from the lap of luxury, this section of Halifax was where the city dumped its undesirable facilities such as a fertilizer plant, slaughterhouses, Rockhead Prison in 1854, and the Infectious Diseases Hospital in the 1870s.

In spite of the lowly services forced upon their neighbourhood and a lack of necessary city services such as electricity, sewers, and garbage disposal—even though they paid taxes—the Black families remained proud. Men got jobs as porters on trains, and ran fishing businesses or farms, as well as small stores. The women kept gardens so their families didn't go hungry.

Africville's first school opened in 1883. There were famous people who came from this part of Canada such as Portia White, the first Canadian concert singer to win international acclaim. Over the decades, little old Africville received such famous visitors as Joe Louis, the boxer, and Stokely Carmichael of the Black Panthers. Such a humble place produced such talented and strong people despite the unfairness, and it was of paramount importance to David that his descendants know this. Know it and prosper with pride and dignity, ever vigilant against similar injustices. David took it upon himself to teach all this to his grandson, Bryan, who was more interested in their family history than his own son William had ever been.

Today was a good day for David because his wife, Ruth, his son William, and his grandson Bryan were coming to visit. He hoped he didn't have to be here longer this time, but they do keep you awhile when you can't breathe from complications of COPD. David was frustrated because this was his second hospitalization in December, and he just wanted to feel better and go home.

"Dad, what the hell's going on here? Someone went missing?" William asked, pulling up a chair to sit by his bed.

"Well, all hell's broken loose, son. There was this old codger like me who just disappeared from his hospital bed last night."

"Language," Ruth said dryly.

"What do you mean by *disappeared*?" Bryan perked up.

"I mean he's gone," David nodded sagely. "Not a bad thing, maybe."

"Meaning...?" Bryan prompted.

"Meaning he wasn't a nice man."

"I know old people are often cranky, but you sound pretty judgy, Dad," William said.

"I know of what I speak, son." David fired a harsh glance at him. "I knew this bastard from years ago - seen him in all kinds of circumstances. Other people can feel sorry for him if they want to, but I don't."

"It's true; he was a bad man." Ruth added.

"Do tell."

Bryan, who had been standing, found another chair and pulled it up to the bedside in one swift motion. He took a swallow of his Red Bull and waited for his grandfather to talk.

"I thought you weren't interested in any of this historical stuff," David said to William.

Looking up, William said, "I am listening now, Dad."

Just then a nurse came in to check David's oxygen tank; they waited patiently for her to leave. David sipped his water through the hospital straw, drawing out the suspense. Finally, he took a deep breath and started talking.

"Cedric was the old man's name. He's been in the Halifax area as long as I have. His family immigrated here from Scotland when he was knee-high to a grasshopper. I've run into him many times over the years because his decisions as a councillor deeply, I mean *deeply*, affected our lives in Africville."

Chapter Two

October

Marie Basque, Louise's mother, sat in an armchair in the living room of Louise and Colin's Halifax home, drumming her fingers on the armrest as she waited for guests to arrive. Louise flitted around, arranging the champagne bottles and the fluted glasses, non-alcoholic beers, and hors d'oeuvres on the kitchen island. She straightened the stack of decorative napkins even though not one had been out of place. Colin fiddled with his Bluetooth speaker and his music app, finally settling on a Classic Rock playlist.

"The banner has fallen down on one side," Marie pointed with an arthritic finger, so Louise stood on a chair to fix the sign decorated with fall leaves of gold, orange, and burgundy. It proclaimed "Engaged! Save the Date - February 14th, 2024!" Colin's colleagues from the police station arrived en masse and rang the doorbell. They spilled into the foyer as soon as he opened the door.

"It's so good to see you all! Everyone, fill up a plate." Louise directed the guests to the food on the table, appetizers, butter tarts, and pumpkin pie. She turned to pass her mother her cane. Marie accepted it but shook her head at Louise's extended arm.

"I can do it myself," she said as she struggled to pull herself up from the soft cushion. "I'll be right back—just have to use the loo." Louise sighed as she watched her mother amble down the hallway to the washroom.

Instead of entering the bathroom, Marie took a left at the guest bedroom which the couple used for extra storage. She opened the drawers of an old dresser and lifted up various out-of-season shorts and swimsuits. She searched the closet where Louise kept her small kitchen appliances, the ones she didn't use every day. Lifting the lid of an Instant Pot, which Louise had said she was thinking of selling, Marie looked inside and found what she had been expecting—a mickey of vodka. Just then, she heard Colin calling out for her, so she slipped the bottle into her deep skirt pocket.

"Coming!" Moving as quickly as an old woman could, she made it to the hallway before her daughter's fiancé rounded the corner.

"Everything okay?" He asked anxiously. It irked Marie when younger people asked her if she was okay when she clearly was. But she knew it was a question asked from caring, so she nodded and worked hard at wiping the annoyance from her face. Colin had known her daughter for years, but was he a good match for her? Louise appreciated that he was hardworking when she herself could be flighty, and strong while Louise struggled at times with anxiety. Marie had some sympathy for him because she knew he'd lost his parents at a young age, but a lifetime of intuition made her doubt him. At times he was too hard on Louise, a bit sharp, snappy.

Then Frankie arrived and greeted Marie with a big hug, careful not to squeeze the older woman too hard.

"So good to see you, Marie!" Frankie looked at Louise and rounded on her for a huge embrace. "My sister from another mother! Congrats!"

Buddy Lamond, whose real name most people didn't even know (it was Robert), introduced himself to Frankie and asked how she knew the family. Louise and Frankie exchanged glances to see who was answering this one. Marie did.

"Frankie came to live with our family when she was seven years old. She was a wonderful complement to our home. We were lucky to have her." Tears sprang to Frankie's eyes, threatening to ruin the mascara she had uncharacteristically applied for the party. She self-consciously sipped her drink to avoid eye-contact with Buddy.

"Mom has always had a soft spot for kids." Louise said, putting her arm around Frankie.

Frankie gestured towards her roommate who stood quietly nearby.

"This is my friend and roommate, Bea."

Bea smiled, shook hands, and thanked Louise for the invitation.

"And how do you know Colin?" Frankie asked Buddy.

Buddy exhaled forcefully, and Colin laughed, clapping him on the shoulder and said, "I've known this guy so long, I forget!" Then, more seriously, Buddy added, "We met at police training, and we've had some crazy times. Never thought I'd see the day when this dude would tie the knot!"

As the sun excused itself for the evening, Edison string lights illuminated the faces of the smiling couple and their guests, as everyone raised a glass in their honour. The only one straight-faced was the one who had known Louise the longest—her mother.

***

Since he got his driver's license earlier that summer, Bryan drove himself to and from his soccer practices and games. Though he loved the freedom that came from borrowing his dad's car, his dad didn't attend as many of his games as he used to, which felt kind of shitty if he was being honest.

One cool evening in the fall, after warming up with his team, the Bedford Bruins, the game against the Halifax Vipers commenced. The two teams were traditionally close in rankings, but that's where any similarities ended. From the south side of Halifax, the Vipers were predominantly Caucasian, preppy, and probably university-bound. In contrast, the Bruins consisted of a mix of new immigrants and long-time Black families who had settled in the area. Sure, some of these young men were also registered for post-secondary studies, but not as surely as those on the other side. There was a time when Bryan wouldn't have made this observation, but that was before he had done his research, understood privilege, educated himself. Thanks to his online friends, he was now aware of injustices he had previously accepted as normal.

On the pitch, he tackled an opponent and the two of them fell to the turf, only to have his calf stepped on by a second Vipers player. Bryan screamed in pain as the offender casually walked off. The opponent he'd tackled hissed at him, "Serves you right, n———-."

"What the..." Bryan gestured at the referee who gave no sign he had heard the insult and signalled him to get up. Bryan refused, and stayed down until the team manager and the coach came out to collect him. His arms around their shoulders, he limped off the field. Was he embellishing? From strictly an injury point of view, yes, but the emotional sting from the slur was real.

"Who was that asshole who stepped on me?" Bryan asked a teammate on the bench as he iced his leg.

"Fucking Owen McCreary. Guy's a dick. Comes from a family of dicks." His teammate clapped him firmly on the shoulder.

Back at the house, Bryan hobbled into the kitchen where his father was sitting reading on his tablet.

"What happened?" His father motioned to a chair at the kitchen table. Bryan shook his head, too furious to sit.

"It's so damn unfair. First he stomps on my leg, then the other jerk-off insults me, and then the ref acts like he didn't see or hear anything."

"Maybe he didn't." As soon as it came out of his mouth, William knew it had been the wrong thing to say. As his son rolled his eyes, he continued, "You could write a strongly worded letter to the soccer association." This was the second-worst thing to say and prompted another eye roll.

"That'd be a waste of time," Bryan said, digging around in the freezer until he located a tub of ice cream. He pulled a large spoon from the drawer, lifted off the lid, and ate straight from the carton.

William raised his eyebrows, but knew not to make a big deal of some bad manners. Ever since his wife, Bryan's mother Portia passed away from cancer a few years ago, his son had floundered. First, his marks had gone down, and then he started vaping. No matter how much Bryan tried to convince his dad that vaping was not as bad as smoking cigarettes, William would not be convinced. But since Bryan's marks had recently come back up, he decided not to bother him anymore about his nicotine habit. Don't poke the bear, he thought. If only Portia were still alive to help him raise this angry young man. Was he being difficult because he'd lost his mother, or was it just normal for his age?

Pointing his spoon at his dad, Bryan said, "You always think you can just pray about things and they'll get better. Or write your city councillor, that kind of bullshit." He shook his head as if giving up on his old man.

William sighed, picked up his tablet and moved into the living room where he settled in his favourite recliner. He knew from experience the boy was spoiling for an argument and he didn't feel like playing along. It was like watching a storm brewing.

Bryan followed his father. "Did writing a letter ever work, Dad? Did it keep Africville from being bulldozed, huh?"

William grimaced and put his earphones in to watch a video. He turned the volume up to drown out his boy, the one he used to like to spend time with, who used to be happy to spend time with him, too. He didn't want to admit that he had also questioned his own pacifist methods.

***

Colin woke up the morning after the engagement party and checked the time on his phone. Six a.m. Beside him, Louise was still asleep. He knew she'd be getting up for work soon, but he had enough time to do what his body demanded. He tiptoed out of the bedroom, closing the door carefully so as not to wake her and padded down the hall to the extra bedroom. He opened the closet and winced as the hinges made a squeak. Reaching into the barely-used Instant Pot, he started, realizing the appliance was empty. It shouldn't have been. He'd left himself a bottle of vodka. What the hell?

Logically, Colin suspected he had an addiction and knew that it was a real taskmaster, but his body wanted it when it wanted it, and if that meant lying to himself and everyone he cared about, then so be it. It's not that he wanted to fool Louise, it's that he *had* to drink.

Puzzled, Colin put the lid back on the pot, and closed the closet door as Louise came out of their bedroom in her housecoat.

"Good morning, sweetie," Louise kissed him on the cheek he dutifully presented. She had trained him not to kiss her on the lips until he had brushed his teeth, and he was a good student. "What were you looking for in there?" she questioned.

"Oh, just wondering if we still had that Instant Pot." He smiled. "Thought I might dig out that cookbook I gave you for Christmas and try out a few recipes."

Louise beamed. "Look at you, getting all domestic and everything. And Buddy said it wouldn't be possible." She kissed his cheek again, and he went back to look for the cookbook. When Louise got into the shower, he went down to the basement bathroom where he took the toilet tank lid off and retrieved another bottle of vodka. He opened it and took deep draughts of straight alcohol as he sat on the toilet lid. He screwed the cap back on, returned the precious bottle to its watery lair, and headed to the kitchen to make the coffee.

***

"I haven't seen my grandson at church for a mighty long time, William." Ruth stood on the sidewalk outside the Baptist church and gestured towards the building as if William didn't know which church she was referring to.

"I know, Ma. Bryan's a teenager. I can't get him to do much of anything lately. He spends most of his time in his room with the door closed, playing games on his computer or whatever."

David put his hand on his wife's forearm. "Don't be too hard on the boy, Ruth. A lot of young men want to be independent, but he knows we're here for him."

"We could come and watch one of his soccer games." Ruth suggested.

"Actually, he quit soccer." William looked around as if hoping some acquaintance would come up and distract his parents.

Their heads swivelled in unison to stare at him.

"Well, he had a run-in with one of the young men on another team and now he doesn't want to go back." He told them the story of the insult and finished with an audible sigh.

"Well, damn," David said. "In my day, that was just the way it was every day all the time. If we'd quit doing what we wanted every time someone called us a name, we'd have stayed in bed all day long never doing nothin'."

Ruth nodded in assent. "You shouldn't have let him quit so impulsively like that."

Then she changed the topic.

"David, remember that time Councillor McCreary came to Africville, and poked around before having the place condemned?"

David nodded gravely. "Sure do. In fact, he had the nerve to come back a week later but changed his mind right quick when me and a bunch of the other men grabbed some baseball bats. We didn't have to use them, but we were ready."

William thought the pride in his father's voice was misplaced. In the end, no one had been able to prevent the demolition of their village. Even the church they were at today wasn't the church they used to attend. That one had been destroyed in the night. *In the night*, as people slept. How thuggish. Sure, a replica of the Seaview Church was built in 2010 accompanied by an apology from the mayor of the day, but it's a museum now, not an operational church. That's the problem with reparations—you can patch something up, but it's never the same.

***

Colin swiped right. He had always loved the thrill of dating apps, the world of possibility in his palm. This woman was just his type: a curvy brunette with long hair, nicely made up, and sexy as hell. Sure, he knew she'd put filters on her profile pic, but he was confident she'd be plenty hot in real life.

The twinge of guilt he felt as an engaged man faded as the exhilaration of sending her a message took over his prefrontal lobe. He hadn't walked down the aisle *yet*. Surely, after the wedding, he'd be ready to settle down and be a one-woman man. In the meantime...

Later that week, Colin looked around the coffee shop for a woman to match the photo. He'd chosen a place in Dartmouth, away from the hospital where Louise worked, away from the stomping grounds of family and friends.

There she was at a table near the window with the pale autumn sun bathing her face. Faith— in her red puffy coat, just as she'd said she'd be—was a vision of loveliness. Colin remembered her photo which showed off her buxom figure currently hidden by her cashmere sweater, revealed as she hung her coat over the back of her chair. When she smiled, she exposed a gap between her front teeth and the beginning of fine lines around her beautiful brown eyes. Colin watched, entranced, as she moved her hair behind her ear and reached out to take his hand in greeting. She was more gorgeous than he'd expected.

During their date, he noticed a dent in her left ring finger—where a ring had obviously been until recently. He wasn't one to judge. Although he'd bought a ring for Louise, he preferred not to wear one himself and had convinced her not to buy him one. He wasn't the kind of guy who blindly followed traditions—and it gave him the clandestine freedom he sought.

In his excitement, he didn't see a slender Indigenous woman a few tables away watching him and Faith. They held hands across their table, busy making plans for their next meeting as Louise's friend, Frankie took care to shield her face as she slipped out the side door of the cafe.

Chapter Three

November

"Bryan, let's go," William knocked on his son's bedroom door. "We talked about this. Grandpa is in the hospital and needs some visitors."

After several minutes, with William just about giving up, Bryan opened the door. William caught a glimpse of the blinds pulled down and clothing tumbling out of open drawers. Strange, his son used to be a tidy person.

On the way to the hospital, Bryan asked, "What happened to Grandpa again?"

William repeated what he had told the boy about David's exacerbated COPD symptoms.

"Your grandparents had it hard in their younger years. They sometimes didn't have enough fresh food to eat. And even if you're not a smoker, that can bring on COPD"

"I thought they were pretty self-sufficient in Africville." Bryan answered.

"Yes, that community worked well for 150 years...until it changed. At first, the government bribed people to leave their homes.

When that didn't work, they intimidated them. One friend of grand-pa's got threats they'd burn his house down. In the end, the city simply brought in bulldozers and took out *completely furnished homes*."

"Unfucking acceptable," muttered Bryan.

"Language." William continued, "Gus Wedderburn, the man who recommended they relocate everyone from Africville, only saw it as a ghetto. He didn't see how the people tried to make their humble homes look nicer. He didn't see the flowers they'd planted or have any idea how hard they worked. Once they were relocated, the people didn't have enough food, no medical care, no possessions, and no community. And there was plenty of racism, which meant no jobs or no *good* jobs."

"Where did they all go when Africville got trashed?"

"Well, that's the problem, isn't it?" William felt anger bubble up in his throat. "They became wards of the state, living in unheated apartments in the bad end of town. These were good people who had never been dependent on the city for anything. Now, everything they had built up was gone, and they were left without the dignity of being able to take care of their families. Years later, Wedderburn was challenged. They showed him a picture of Africville with neatly kept yards and gardens filled with beautiful blooms. All he could say in his defense was, "I didn't see the flowers." It was a crying shame."

They pulled into the parking lot for the Geriatric Restorative Care Unit, picked up some muffins from the coffee shop, and took the elevator to David's floor.

As they walked past a patient's room, Bryan stopped short. He recognized a voice. As he suspected, it belonged to Owen McCreary, the bastard who'd stepped on his leg on purpose. Even though Mc-Creary had his back to him, the guy's physique had imprinted on his mind like some kind of warning mechanism. Turns out that prick's grandpa was sick, too. He shook his head to dislodge any fraternal feelings for this horrible person. Peering past Owen, he caught sight of a wizened old man sitting up in bed with a large bandage on one leg.

"Come on," William had stopped, and was looking back quizzically at his son. Bryan took a moment to see where Cedric McCreary's room (22) was in relation to his grandfather's and caught up with his dad.

***

As an introvert, Frankie didn't mind cleaning at the hospital so much as having to interact with the patients sometimes just to be polite—especially in the geriatric wing where so many of them were lonely and wanted to talk to anyone with a pulse or even without.

The elderly man in Room 22 looked to be asleep, which Frankie noted with relief. No awkward banter this time. She quietly moved the broom around the baseboards and was using the dustpan when she heard a rustling sound coming from the bed.

As the man sat up slowly, he said, "Do they really let you injuns work here?"

Frankie froze, unsure of how to respond to what she'd just plainly heard.

As if taking that as a sign to continue, he went on in a faux-polite voice, "I mean, shouldn't you be on the reservation?" He drew out each syllable of the last word for effect.

Out of the corner of her eye, Frankie registered movement at the door. It was a teenage boy with an afro. He rounded the door frame, holding onto it with one hand and swinging his body into the room in one smooth motion, graceful and strong.

"Is this old fuck bothering you?" He looked at Frankie with bright eyes.

The elderly man's jaw fell open as it might in a melodrama, an exaggerated but spontaneous expression of surprise.

"Uh…" Frankie's instinct was to freeze, to play down the old man's insult, but something deep down told her not to this time. "Yes, he *is* bothering me."

The solid presence of this furious young man gave her a fortitude she'd never felt before. She glanced at the door to see if anyone else was around.

Before she knew it, Bryan approached the bed and made as if to straighten the top sheet for Cedric. Instead, he leaned in and whispered something in Cedric's wrinkled ear. Frankie couldn't hear what, but Cedric, already pale, turned corpse-white and sat stone-still. Giving Cedric's bandaged stump, the place where his foot used to be, a little squeeze, and eliciting a yelp, Bryan escorted Frankie rather gallantly from the room. For a moment she felt so grateful she thought she might be in love (even though he was just a boy), and she watched him as he moved away down the hall until he turned into the room where his grandfather sat with his oxygen tank. Frankie was unaware that William, who had gone back for coffee, stood behind her in the hallway with a cup of coffee in each hand, peering into Room 22. He moved unobtrusively past her. Then Cedric wailed, and Frankie stood holding her broom like a staff as a nurse rushed past her to check on the old fart.

A few days later, David was released from hospital and William wanted his son to come along for dinner at his parent's favourite restaurant to celebrate. He knocked on Bryan's bedroom door to let him know it was time to leave.

Bryan opened the door a crack and looked suspiciously at his father.

"We're off," William said, gesturing toward the door.

"I'm not coming," Bryan started to close the door on his dad.

Frustrated, William said, "Why not? You've got to eat anyway, son."

"I'm not hungry. Anyway, I'm busy." The door closed. William stood there for a few minutes, took a few deep breaths, and left.

Bryan logged into his usual chat room.

"So much happened today, bro." As he wrote to his friend, Yusra, he described in detail his earlier run-in with Owen McCreary on the soccer pitch.

"So I quit the team a couple of months ago. No way I'm dealing with that loser anymore." Yusra approved, but a niggling voice in the back of his mind reminded Bryan his dad had encouraged him to keep playing and maybe he should have. He didn't like to see himself as a quitter.

"Son," his dad had said, "there are a lot of difficult people in this world, but you shouldn't let them take your fun away."

When he told Yusra about his encounter with Owen's grandfather at the hospital and squeezing Cedric's stump, his online buddy typed a laugh emoji, but asked what "injun" meant.

"It's a slur against Indigenous people."

"What does indigenous mean?" Yusra asked. For the first time, Bryan wondered where Yusra lived. Not North America, obviously. Uneasily, it occurred to him that he hadn't told his grandpa or his dad about his encounter with Cedric. Even though he'd been standing up for the janitor, he suspected his family wouldn't be proud of the way he'd done it.

Chapter Four

Early December

"Excuse me, I have to attend to my patient," Louise said to the woman visiting Cedric McCreary. "Can you step outside, please?"

"It's ok, she can stay. She's my wife." Cedric said weakly. Louise glanced at the young, attractive brunette sitting in the chair beside his bed. "She used to be really poor, but now she has a very nice life with me."

"That's nice, sir, but I need to concentrate, and it's just easier." Louise waited patiently as the woman stood up and collected her designer purse. Cedric has definitely robbed the cradle, she thought as the clacking of his wife's heels receded in the hallway.

"How long have you been married?" She tried not to let her curiosity show too much.

"Six months. We're practically newlyweds! My dear Faith." Louise figured he must have tons of money because he was well into his nineties, and no matter how handsome he might have been at one time, he was as old as dirt now, and quite sick.

"By the way, can I get put on a different floor?" He turned on what he must have thought was a charming smile. To Louise, it looked like a rictus.

"Well, you already have your own private room in geriatrics. What's the problem?" She asked.

He looked around as if about to impart an important top-secret morsel of information. "There are a lot of coloreds on this floor." Cedric implored with a complicit half-smile. Louise wanted to drop kick the old bastard in the chest.

"Excuse me?" She said frostily.

He wiped the creepy grin off his face and rearranged his droopy features into an imploring look. "Oh no, that didn't come out right. Forget I said anything."

As Louise finished up with the dressings on his amputated foot, his wife returned with two take-out cups.

"Coffee for my Cedric!" She announced, setting his beverage down on the tray, sweeping away the items already on it, sending a bottle of eye drops onto the bed. Louise cringed at Faith's sing-song voice, not quite baby talk, but not far off. She left the room without saying goodbye.

When visiting hours were over, Cedric fell asleep. The hospital churned out countless beeping noises and announcements, but being hard of hearing, his sleep was undisturbed. Being deaf also meant that when someone stealthily entered Room 22, he didn't know what hit him, had no time to react, as the assailant struck his thin body hard and repeatedly as he lay prone under the covers.

***

The next day, the city was abuzz with news of the attack. Frankie overheard two passengers on the bus talking about an assault on a patient at the geriatric centre. Upon opening the storage room, she searched for her broom. It wasn't where she'd left it. What a pain—she'd have to go to one of the other floors and borrow another if it wasn't being used. Her work gloves were missing, too. She'd spent her own money on those and hoped they'd turn up soon. These brooms gave her slivers if she didn't wear gloves.

On the floor below the old folks' floor, Frankie waited at the reception desk for someone to help her but they were all busy. Her ears perked up to hear tight whispers coming from a couple near the elevator.

"Why did you *do* that?" A beautiful, dark-haired woman hissed at a rough-looking man in workwear. She had an accent of some sort, was she Filipina maybe? As far as Frankie knew, the man didn't work at the hospital unless he had just recently been hired in maintenance.

His eyes darted around, as if making sure no one was paying attention to them.

Frankie fiddled with a pen on the counter to look busy.

"I didn't do nothin'," he hissed. Frankie read his lips rather than actually hearing him. The woman looked doubtful. Then the two of them got on the elevator, so Frankie learned no more, but she did register that the woman's abdomen was gently rounded. And finally she was able to borrow some gloves and a broom for her shift.

***

One of the tasks Frankie had at this time of year was to put up the Christmas tree on the geriatric floor, so today was a welcome change from her usual drudgery. She got some help from a male coworker to bring the large, heavy tree out of storage and assemble it. The decorating was the easy part, and she quite enjoyed doing it herself.

"Looking good," Louise said as she stopped by to admire her handiwork.

"Thanks," Frankie blushed, knowing that she still hadn't been able to bring herself to tell Louise about seeing Colin at the coffee shop with that woman. Work didn't seem to be the right time. Maybe next weekend when they were going out to the rez to visit her dad.

Frankie reached into her pocket and brought out a small, beaded tree decoration, which she placed on the front of the tree at eye level. Louise stopped and took a closer look. It was a medicine wheel created from seed beads in white, black, yellow and red.

Lifting it gently, Louise asked, "Did you make this?" Frankie nodded and Louise patted her on the arm before saying goodbye for the evening. With a warm glow in her heart, Frankie tidied up. She wasn't sure what to do with the large canvas bag the tree had been stored in, so she tucked it under a nearby table against the wall which had a floor-length tablecloth on it. The bag was out of sight and out of mind, except that someone had watched Frankie put it there.

***

For the investigation into the beating of Cedric McCreary, Colin and Buddy had the use of some empty offices in the hospital administration wing. They divided up the interviews between them. The old man's wife, his son, and his grandson were swarming the lobby until Buddy firmly insisted they wait until called.

"That family's chomping at the bit to get justice." Buddy muttered and shook his head.

Colin sat down heavily on a chair and wiped a clammy brow with his forearm. "Hey, Buddy, congrats on being the lead on this case."

"Thanks, man." Then he asked, "You okay?"

"Yeah, it's just hot in here," Colin replied.

"It's *not* hot in here, man. If anything they could turn up the damn heat." Buddy said, staring hard at his partner.

"The wife, Faith, she's broken up about this." Colin changed the subject. "After Louise and Frankie, we still have to interview her, the doctor, and the maintenance man. You take the wife; I'll interview the doctor, and whoever's finished first can interview the other guy." Colin attempted a casual tone, but was panicking inside about seeing Faith again in this situation. They'd only hooked up a few times and then he'd ghosted her. It was super-awkward, and he just wanted to avoid her.

Buddy nodded, and then said in a lowered voice, "Hey, have you been drinking?"

Colin started to protest but interrupted himself by vomiting violently into a garbage can.

"Jesus, Colin. I thought you quit drinking! You look like shit. Fuck! Don't make me report you, man, 'cause I will."

"No, don't!" Colin pleaded. "I *did* quit. I'll quit again—I promise."

Buddy shook his head as he left the room. "See that you do."

Buddy led Louise to a nearby room and motioned to a chair where she could sit at a small table across from him. "Colin's too close to you, obviously, " he smiled apologetically, "so I get to interview you." Louise nodded before explaining that she didn't really know much other than to describe Cedric's bruises in detail.

"Whoever hit him was fairly strong and probably angry," she offered.

"Did he have any visitors yesterday?"

Louise looked up as she recalled. "His wife was the only visitor I saw here yesterday."

"Did you see anything suspicious?"

Louise thought carefully. "No," she finally said because she hadn't. Should she mention the old man's casual racism? It made her furious. Could someone else have overheard it? Cedric McCreary probably had a habit of talking like that. Maybe a lot of people hated him enough to beat him. This was just speculation though, so in the end, Louise remained quiet. Well, she thought wryly, he got his wish to be moved to a different floor—the ICU. Though she didn't consider herself a vengeful person, she felt that Cedric got exactly what he deserved.

After Buddy interviewed Louise, he faced Cedric's wife, furious son and equally unpleasant grandson. Faith sat primly in the corner, dabbing at her eyes with a tissue, while Cedric's son fumed. "I've contacted a lawyer and we're going to sue this hospital for everything it's worth!" As if his entitled attitude wasn't hard enough to take, the grandson lay draped like some drunken prince across a chair. He wanted to slap that shit-eating grin right off the boy's face.

Meanwhile, Colin bought himself a Gatorade from the vending machine in the hall and then called the custodian into the room. Frankie sat on her hands, a habit she'd picked up in order to not bite her fingernails. He thought it made her look childlike, vulnerable. Noticing she had a hard time making eye contact, he looked warily at her and pointed to a wood-handled broom and a set of work gloves, the kind with rubberized fingers.

"Do you recognize these?"

Her eyes darted from the items to his face. Why does he look so pasty, she wondered. "Yes. That's the broom I usually use and my own gloves. I looked for them earlier, but they weren't in the supply closet where I left them.

"That's because they were in the dumpster behind this building." His tone sounded accusing to Frankie.

"Oh," she frowned. "Can I have them back? I borrowed a broom from the floor below, but they'll want it back. And I paid for those gloves myself."

Colin shook his head and said bluntly. "No, these are evidence now." Frankie felt her stomach drop. Her supplies were evidence? Even though she hadn't been on shift last night, she had no one to corroborate that she was in her apartment in Dartmouth. Bea had been out. Was this going to end up badly for her? Colin dismissed her and it was all she could do not to run out of the room.

***

When the apartment doorbell rang, Frankie pressed the intercom to ask who was at the door; her heart sank. It was a Halifax policeman.

She invited him in, but the officer declined, remaining at the door. She was being summoned to appear in court, charged with aggravated assault in the beating of Cedric McCreary. With her pulse pounding in her ears, she accepted the paperwork and closed the door behind the officer. What now? She sunk down to the floor with her back against the door.

After a cry, Frankie called Marie. She'd have preferred to call Louise, but she knew she was on shift. Marie picked up the phone and Frankie explained her situation.

"Oh, Frankie, I'm so sorry." The woman who had mothered her all her life was there to support her.

"What do I do?" Frankie wailed.

"You need to get a lawyer. You're Indigenous, so you'll qualify for legal aid. What evidence do they have on you?" Marie asked.

"Well, it *was* my gloves and the broom that he was beaten with."

"That seems pretty circumstantial," Marie mused.

"I don't know. I'll have to look at these documents and see what I have to do next. At least I'm allowed to stay in my apartment until the court date, but I have a curfew."

Marie offered to accompany Frankie to court.

"Honestly, child, let me support you. None of this is easy."

This gesture was so kind it made Frankie bawl.

***

The day after Cedric's beating, William and Bryan had dropped over to David and Ruth's apartment. William had insisted his son apologize for missing their dinner out. When they arrived, the news of the beating was blaring on the TV. They watched together, trying to learn what would have happened right under their very noses if David hadn't been released.

"What's with your hands?" David pointed at the bandaids on William's palms.

"Oh, this. It's nothing. Just used my shovel on the driveway this morning without gloves and got some blisters."

Bryan turned to his grandfather. "At least we know *you* didn't beat the old guy."

"He had it coming." William muttered, almost to himself.

"Geez, Son." David shot him a look.

Bryan looked at his dad, usually so mild-mannered, and wondered if he had a mean streak after all. He wasn't sure which version of his dad he liked better. Now that he came to think of it, his dad had *not* shovelled the driveway that morning. Why did his old man lie?

Back home, Bryan made a bee-line for his bedroom and turned on his laptop. He was aware that he could only be away from his computer for a few hours, then craved to connect again with Yusra and the others. He wondered about the circumstances of Yusra's life. Did he have brothers? Sisters? Had anyone he loved died of cancer like Bryan's mother had? As much as he wanted to know, it wasn't something he felt comfortable asking. But he couldn't wait to share what had happened at the hospital.

In his darkened room, his face bathed in the blue light of his laptop screen, he logged into the chatroom he'd found through social media, the one that made sense to him, the one about getting justice for racism, and not in the slow, useless way his dad tried (writing your city councillor and that kind of bullshit). No, his new friends spoke of resistance and even violence, not in the distant future, but *right now.*

When Bryan typed into the group chat what had happened to Cedric McCreary, one of them responded, "That's the only thing some people understand—pain."

"I'm so glad I found you guys," Bryan typed. "You really get me. My dad doesn't get me at all." He waited a moment, then Yusra replied..

"I always have a listening ear for you, my friend. Soon it will be time to act. Revolution."

***

A week later, Cedric McCreary was out of the ICU and back in the geriatric wing, much to Louise's dismay. She made herself smile, fake though it felt, as she entered his private room.

"Good morning, Mr. McCreary."

He nodded solemnly. "Had a bit of a rough go there."

"Yes, hopefully the police will get to the bottom of it in no time," she replied, attempting a sympathy she didn't feel.

"At least I got some good news," he said, perking up visibly.

"Oh?" Louise was only half-listening as she checked his fluids.

"Faith, my wife, is pregnant!" He beamed ear to ear, looking like the proverbial cat who caught the canary. Louise just about dropped the bedpan.

She recovered quickly and said, "Well, congratulations, Mr McCreary!" The same sing-song voice Faith had used floated out of her own mouth.

Leaving the room, she shut the door behind her and exhaled. Could this old bastard actually have any swimming sperm left? How far along was Faith? Speak of the devil, she thought as Faith came down the hallway toward Cedric's room, her shapely hips swaying as she walked. She wasn't alone though. There was a maintenance man with her. Or maybe they weren't together, Louise thought, as the guy took a left turn down a hall. *Was* he a maintenance man? She hadn't had time to notice whether he wore a lanyard ID. Sneaking a glance at the woman, she thought she could just make out a small baby bump, but when would Faith and Cedric have had sex? He'd been in the hospital for weeks, and she thought there's no way this man's 94 year-old seed made a baby. No way.

Chapter Five

Middle of December

After setting up the tent, Frankie started a fire with twigs and used her ax to split some of the dry firewood from under the tarp. She'd gone hunting with her cousins a few times but had to admit to herself that they had done most of the actual work. She sat on a log and opened a granola bar. Its wrapper made an outsized crackling sound in the quiet of the forest, which caused her to wonder about dangerous wildlife. As a child, she'd heard stories of coy wolves, part wolf and part coyote which sounded like some kind of mythical beast. A Google search revealed that they did indeed exist, but there weren't any in Nova Scotia. Eastern coyotes, on the other hand, were a distinct possibility. She'd have to be careful and watch herself. As the sun set, she gazed up as the stars slowly winked into view.

Frankie slept fitfully, disturbed by every sound no matter how slight. Finally, she gave up and got up, feeling the effects of the deep drop in temperature. Wishing she had cell phone coverage, or even an old-school watch to tell the time, she guessed by the stars it was about two or three in the morning. Shivering, she slipped on her boots and went out to poke at the near-dead fire with a stick. A few embers glowed as she stirred them to life, adding more kindling and wood. She sat so close to it, she could smell the plastic on her boots overheating, but she didn't care. The stars continued their path across the sky. As the fire dwindled, Frankie slumped over and drifted off to sleep.

***

If the city was stunned the day Cedric was beaten, it positively *exploded* when the news broke that the elderly man who had been beaten in his hospital bed had now *disappeared*. Just what was going on at the geriatric centre? A nurse had checked on McCreary around three a.m. only to find his bed empty. A thorough search of the hospital revealed nothing. Cedric's room was cordoned off and the place was crawling with police officers and detectives.

On the same floor, a male nurse paused outside a supply closet because he heard voices coming from within. He was going to use his card to open the door, but then decided to listen in instead.

"Why did you move him? It wasn't necessary." A female voice sounded near hysteria, hoarse.

"It's better that way. Don't worry, they won't feckin' find him where I left him. Won't be able to examine him," answered a man in a harsh whisper. Newfoundland accent? the nurse wondered.

With a muffled sob, the woman continued, "No! You shouldn't have! He was *old*. They probably expected him to die any day anyway. You should've just left him there."

"Actually, luv, there's a different problem. That nurse, the tall one, she saw me take the Christmas tree bag out from under the table. I have to do something about *her* now."

"Nooo." The woman wept softly.

Not sure what to make of the conversation, the nurse walked away, but knew he had to find a police officer to report what he heard. It sure sounded suspicious.

Later that day, hours after sunset and after missing his scheduled shift at work at the job he'd never return to, a man waited in the hospital parkade. He'd been keeping an eye on Louise for a while, knew she was on the later shift and where she parked her car. She should be along any minute, he figured.

Hearing footsteps, he ducked between cars and saw Louise getting her key fob ready. He was glad she had a newer vehicle and not an old one which comes with metal keys. Women had been told for years to stab a potential attacker in the eye with those.

***

Concerned about the frigid temperatures, Ujil and Joan set out in the weak light of dawn to search for Frankie. As Joan suspected, she was at her secret campsite. They found her on the ground in front of the remains of the fire. Her father knelt and quickly began shaking her awake.

Frankie dreamed of warm hands. "Mmm, coyote... mom..." She slurred unintelligible nonsense words.

"Oh geez," Ujjl looked up at Joan in alarm. "She's talkin' funny."

"She probably has hypothermia. Let's get her back and warmed up."

They awkwardly hoisted Frankie onto the old toboggan, wrapped her in a blanket Joan had brought along, and pulled her back to the house.

"Should I heat up some water on the stove?" Ujjl asked, once they had laid Frankie on his bed. Joan shook her head.

"No, it's better if we warm her up more gently, say with an electric blanket. Do you have one?" Ujjl shook his head sadly. "It's ok, Jim. I do. I'll run back to my place and get it. In the meantime, I need you to take your shirt off."

"What?" His eyes goggled.

"No, nothing like that. The best way to warm her is skin-to-skin contact." Joan was already peeling off Frankie's shirt, leaving her only in her bra and sweatpants. The sight of his daughter's body, that of a young woman now, made Ujjl's eyes tear up. He hadn't seen her, hadn't really *looked* at his child in years. She'd grown up, and he'd missed it. Time to take off his damn shirt, he thought. Time to step up. He did so, and lay down beside her, rolling her onto her side so they could spoon. The coldness of her skin, its pallor alarmed him, and he wept.

Frankie slept on and off throughout the day as Ujjl and Joan took turns giving her sips of water and chicken broth and her father kept the wood stove burning. As she improved, she ate some toast at the kitchen table.

"How long have I been out of it?" She asked.

"We found you early this morning, so a few hours, for sure."

"Ujjl, I'm so sorry I ran away and didn't go to the hospital with you. Are you okay?"

Her father reached out for her hand. "I did have a seizure, but I'll be fine," and added, "and you'll be fine, too."

"I tried to take some time for myself, but it went sideways. Now I have to get back to Halifax. Some serious shit is going down."

They both protested, saying she needed to stay and get her strength back

"Don't rush. Nothing's happening that fast in the case of that old man," Joan said, and Ujjl nodded in agreement. As if to put paid to that lie, Frankie turned on the TV, and the news was still all about the disappearance of Cedric McCreary. She felt the familiar tentacles of anxiety branching out from her stomach to her chest, reaching around her heart, squeezing .

"I dread talking to the cops, but maybe the sooner I do it, the sooner they'll leave me alone." Her father and Joan tried to convince her why she shouldn't leave—it's too dark for driving, tomorrow's soon enough, she might faint while driving—but to no avail.

"I need to talk to Louise, too. I owe her an apology."

Frankie showered, packed her clothes, and hugged them both goodbye.

At the same time, in Halifax, Colin was staggering out of a pub where he'd had more than a few drinks. In his current state, he judged that he was fine to drive his Jeep home.

***

Thankful for clear roads, Frankie made good time. Instead of going home, she headed to the hospital and found a spot in the near-empty parkade. She rested her head against the steering wheel with closed eyes. She needed to give herself a little pep talk to go inside. Time to get this over with. She'd find out from her coworkers what was new on Cedric McCreary's disappearance, and if the police were still onsite, she would talk to them, too.

She opened her eyes and looked up just in time to see Louise get in her car. Probably finished her shift and on her way home, Frankie thought, deciding she could apologize to her tomorrow. Suddenly, the headlights of a nearby truck lit up. The driver wore a black coat with the hood up, so it was hard to see what the person looked like although the general vibe was male. It gave her an uneasy feeling. She looked back to see that Louise was already driving toward the exit. Frankie panicked to see the truck begin to follow behind. She started her vehicle and joined the unintentional convoy.

Frankie followed at what she hoped was a safe distance. As she approached Louise's house, she sure didn't want the driver to notice her, so she parked a few houses away, turned off her lights, and hunkered down in her seat. As Louise pulled into her driveway, the man in the truck, who had parked on the street ahead of Frankie, got out of his car and opened the gate at the back of his truck. Dialling 911 with trembling fingers, Frankie watched helplessly as he moved stealthily toward her friend, who was getting her bag from the backseat of the car, a long piece of wood clenched in his hand. He's stalking her like a wild cat, Frankie thought, watching him approaching Louise who had yet to see him. Frankie was too far away to yell for her attention.

Sobbing, she gave the address to the 911 dispatcher who told her to stay put. Frankie shrieked as she saw the assailant hit her friend over the head and crumple to the ground. The noise was sickening and Frankie interrupted her crying to retch.

She cried, "He's putting her in the back of his truck!" The attacker did so as if loading cordwood, put up the door, and sped off.

Frankie peeled away from the curb and drove after the attacker, devastated at the thought of Louise rolling around unconscious in the back of that truck. "Ohmygod, ohmygod, ohmygod," she muttered and then realized the 911 operator was still talking to her.

"He's taking her down Windsor Street," Frankie told the disembodied voice on the line. "Wait a minute..." A blue vehicle made a sudden right-hand turn into her lane forcing Frankie to brake hard.

Swearing, she watched the truck ahead turn right at the corner and slow down. Why would a perp slow down with someone chasing him? Before she could think of an answer, the SUV plowed right into the back of the truck at high speed, pushing it a dozen feet forward. The crash was deafening. Frankie couldn't make out what the operator was saying.

"What the hell?" She thought dizzily. Didn't the driver see that the guy in the truck had stopped? Why was he even here? Oh my God, Louise! Frankie sat transfixed in her car and just managed to turn it off before passing out.

When she came to, there were police cars everywhere. She tried to sit up from the gurney the paramedics had put her on in the back of an ambulance.

"Lie back. You're in shock."

Before obeying, she watched first responders put the SUV driver on a stretcher to load him into another ambulance. She turned her head to get a look at the driver's face. To her shock and dismay, it was Colin Doughty—Louise's fiancé! Then Frankie overheard an officer say the perpetrator had escaped on foot into the Fairview Lawn Cemetery and that police officers were stationed at various points to catch him. From what she'd seen of the attacker's MO, Frankie's money was on the perp.

"Frankie, is that you?" She opened her eyes to see Buddy, the police officer who she had met at Louise's engagement party kneeling beside her. She nodded weakly.

"How's Louise?" The word was uttered with effort through chapped lips.

Buddy said nothing, his mouth a thin, flat line. He shook his head.

Frankie's face crumpled. "I didn't even get a chance to apologize to her." She started to cry, "and what do we tell Marie?"

Buddy reached out to hold her hand, which had an IV attached. "The truth, Frankie. Once we figure out what that is."

Chapter Six

Late December

Darnell Smith, who's name wasn't really Darnell, felt the adrenaline rush he knew so well from all the other times he was up to no good. It started as a jolt in his chest and exploded to his extremities, the fight or flight sensation that some people hate but he thrived on.

Having worked at the hospital for a few months, he now had the lay of the land, knew which nurses were on night shift and when they went for breaks. This made it a fun challenge for him to slip into the old man's room unseen. He found that if you had some tools on you and wore a uniform, no one questioned your presence anywhere in the building at any time.

Poking Cedric McCreary's shoulder in the half-dark, he waited for a response but none came. Darnell reached down and opened one crepey eyelid, the pupils were dilated. Darnell was no doctor, but a cursory feel for a pulse turned up nothing and a hand at the mouth revealed no breath. The old man's lips and fingernails were blue, and his skin felt cold. Darnell quickly unzipped the large bag he had pulled out earlier that day from under the table in the hall, the one the Christmas tree had been stored in. It was from a big box store and had plenty of room for a shrunken, old corpse.

Getting McCreary in there was trickier than he had anticipated, his experience was more of the break-and-enter variety. The geezer's body wasn't that flexible, but he managed to fold him into it anyway. This was his first murder/body disposal, but he was up for it—something different; you know, keep it fresh. Darnell opened the door and saw a nurse at the station at the end of the hallway. He waited inside the doorway peeking out periodically until she had her back to him, charting. At least she wasn't coming this way, he thought as he slipped down the stairwell with the bag. "I'm a Grinch of sorts," he chuckled to himself.

He put on a black coat with a hood that he had stuffed on top of the body and zipped up the jacket to hide his uniform which had been useful while inside. He then pushed the back door open hard. It opened onto the parking lot where he'd left his truck. In case of cameras, he moved slowly as though he were merely putting an artificial Christmas tree into the truck bed like so many other Canadians in December. Nothing to see here.

Inside his truck, he set his GPS for Hants County where he knew there were many peat bogs. He had prepped a road trip snack of Red Bulls and chips for his hour-long ride. Playlist at the ready, he steered his Ford F150 out of the lot and headed north nodding his head in time to Metallica.

After an uneventful ride—not much traffic in the wee hours of the night in the winter—Darnell pulled off the highway onto a rural road which he followed for several kilometres. When he came to a stop, he left his headlights on, confident that no one was around out in the boonies at this hour. Digging in a knapsack, he located his headlamp, put it on over a warm hat, and turned it on.

Rounding the outside of the truck, he lowered the back door and pulled the heavy bag toward himself. Opening the zipper, he shrieked as a veiny hand, surprisingly strong, grabbed his wrist. Darnell jumped back, yanking his arm away and swore in a higher voice than he had known he could make. He punched reflexively, wildly, at the old man who was crawling blindly out of the bag. To Darnell's dismay, Cedric, although no match for the younger man, hit back and managed to land a few of his own. Although it was all a blur, Darnell registered that Cedric was doing this all on arthritic knees and without being able to see well. The strikes didn't hurt much, but Darnell sure as hell felt it when Cedric plunged his long-nailed thumb into his eye socket. He cried out, stepped back to regroup, and then jumped right into the truck bed with Cedric, shouting and grabbing the old man by the throat. It was like fighting a wounded animal, and Darnell squeezed until the old man's bulging eyes glazed over, reminding him of a dead frog's eyes. Though he was sure he must be dead, he hung on longer just in case. He'd seen a lot of horror movies where the zombies just won't *die*. Finally, he let go, and the former councillor slumped forward, unmoving.

"Holy shit," Darnell took out his vape with shaking hands and had a few puffs to calm himself. Faith had given the old goat a good dose of poison earlier that night. She'd done a lot of research online about milligrams and body weight. What she'd put in his tea should've been enough to finish him off. What the hell? He looked down at his hands, hands that had just strangled an old man.

Well, he thought, time's a-tickin'. His phone screen glowed, and he read the time as two a.m. with his good eye as the other one throbbed. Without further delay, he forced the body back into the bag. Before zipping it up, he remembered that he wanted to leave a misleading clue with the body in case it was ever discovered. He tucked an ornament he'd plucked from the hospital Christmas tree into the bag. It was a beaded circle in black, white, red, and yellow, evenly stitched and backed with hide. Indigenous. Nice work.

Darnell put on a pair of rubber boots and tucked his pants into them. He pulled the bag out of the back and it landed with a thud on the ground. Dragging the body, he picked his way through the dark bog marsh aiming his footfalls for the drier parts of the ground. Stranded on a clump, he cursed the limitations of his headlamp. He could see a few feet around himself and it was all sodden ground. Maybe if he jumped he could reach a drier area about six feet away.

Cedric's dead weight, thin though the old man had been, was enough to throw Darnell's jump off course. He *almost* made it but ended up with one leg on the dry grass and the other leg thigh-deep in mud. Darnell had never been flexible, so this position was rather uncomfortable to say the least, kind of like doing a standing scissor kick but just holding it. Repeated attempts to pull out his lower leg resulted in only a slurping sound, but not much movement. Darnell panted and sweated, wondering what time it was. He needed to be out of here by sunrise.

"Maybe I should throw something onto the grass so if someone comes looking for me they'll know where I went down." He rummaged frantically in his coat pockets coming up only with his vape and keys. Then he realized that if anyone found him that would actually be *bad*. How could he possibly explain his presence out here? But what if he couldn't get out, and nobody rescued him, and he just fucking died here? Strangely, he also realized he couldn't ever part with either his nicotine or his truck. He slowly replaced both items in his pockets.

Yelling and fighting back tears, Darnell heaved his upper body forward in a forced fall over and over again, eventually touching grass that had, until now, been just out of his reach. It was tall enough for him to grab and get enough traction to slowly pull himself out. The quicksand-like mud closed over his boot like wet cement – gone for good. Exhausted, Darnell lay gasping on the turf for several minutes. All he knew was that he had to get rid of this body and make it safely back to his truck as soon as possible. He decided that the mud he'd just extricated himself from was as good a spot as any, so he pushed the bag until it was completely submerged. Darnell turned around and heaved it into the morass from which he'd just emerged. He watched, transfixed, as it sank quickly, black muck evenly covering it over. Gathering his remaining strength of which there was little, and his courage of which there was even less, he leaped back across the wet expanse, successful this time without Cedric's added weight. Aware that his bare foot was freezing, he carefully hobbled back to his truck.

Inside the cab, he tossed the headlamp on the floor, cranked the heat up and used his beanie to wipe some of the mud from his frozen foot before reversing his vehicle and heading home. He had to squint because he'd also gotten some bog mud in his left eye.

Chapter Seven

Part 2 - January 2024

David Kennedy was happy his second stint in the hospital had so far not resulted in a third. Christmas had come and gone without incident. Getting to keep the oxygen tank was a bonus for him, as well as for Ruth's peace of mind. That said, he hadn't slept well since the beating and subsequent disappearance of Cedric McCreary from the very floor they had both occupied. Something else was bothering him, too.

"How's Bryan doing," he asked his son. "Still spending too much time on the computer?"

William, who had come for a New Year's visit, nodded unhappily.

"Well, if he keeps that up, he's going to have mental health issues," Ruth added. Rather unhelpfully, William thought.

He sighed. Bryan's marks in school had dropped again, but more than that, William didn't want to tell his parents about the package he'd recently intercepted addressed to Bryan, the one containing a tactical vest and a ballistic helmet, of all things. After doing nothing about it for a few days, trying to convince himself that it was nothing to worry about, William finally reached out to the RCMP and reported his son, *his own damn son*. He felt a mixture of emotions, shame for betraying Bryan, absolute fear for the boy's mental health, and anger that Bryan could possibly be planning something dangerous and illegal. Was this the result of all that time spent online? William had wanted to believe Bryan had been playing games, but it now seemed his son had been delving into something much more sinister. Lately, Bryan got excited every time the doorbell rang. Little did the kid know he wasn't getting his package but something a lot more complicated.

***

The night of the chase, Darnell had run from his truck, abandoning Louise in the back of it, sprinted through the cemetery and flagged down a cab. It had been such bad luck for his truck to stall when it did. It could have been the end of the road for him. How was he to know that he was being followed? No way he was going to prison, he vowed. The cab dropped him off at his brother Harold's apartment (everyone called him Bubbles), and Darnell talked him into driving him all the way to Labrador. He sweetened the deal by offering a large chunk of the money that would be coming his way from Faith now that her old fart husband was gone. Labrador City isn't the asshole of the world, but you can see it from there, he thought. It was, however, a good place to disappear for a while, and he could get a job at the mine. The plan was to get Faith and their baby out there shortly.

***

As the search for McCreary morphed into a recovery mission, Buddy and his team worked with the RCMP and their cadaver dogs to search an increasingly larger radius around Halifax to find the body.

A boggy area about an hour and a bit north of the city had promise. Sure enough, on a dreary, cold, late-January morning, investigators found a large faded red bag containing human remains floating on the surface of a peat bog.

"How come the body's not buried?" Buddy asked one of the RCMP officers who was only too happy to explain.

"Oh, it's because of the peat content. With this much spaghnum, look how the water surface is trapped under all these stems and leaves. That restricts the temperature exchange between the water and the air, meaning that even if the perp had weighted the body, it still would've floated to the surface after three or four days."

According to Buddy's calculations, Cedric's corpse had been missing for at least four weeks. Although cold temperatures and peat had slowed its decomposition, it definitely looked like an elderly male. Dental records would likely confirm its identity.

Louise's body, on the other hand, had been easy to identify. It was the saddest thing for her mother to have to do—and right before Christmas, too. Poor Louise hadn't had a chance in hell when Colin's Jeep rammed into the back of that truck. Not a sweet hope.

"I found this in the bag with the body." The RCMP handed a small, dirty object to Buddy who accepted it with gloved hands.

"Looks like a beaded piece." Buddy muttered to himself as he examined it, peering closely without overhandling. It had seed beads of red, yellow, white and black. "It's got a loop on top for hanging on something." He shook his head and placed it in a plastic evidence bag, and then put the red bag with the remains in a large black body bag.

***

The last time Buddy saw Frankie was at Louise's funeral. Although Louise hadn't been religious as far as he knew, there had been a mass and funeral, and no doubt it had brought comfort to Marie. Sitting near the aisle at the back, Buddy could just make out Frankie passing Kleenex to the woman and putting her arm around her. Many of the hospital staff were there. Some of the crowd looked like Louise and Colin's friends, the ones who had been at the engagement party, but he didn't remember their names. Colin was nowhere to be found, but Buddy knew why that was. You can't be in a hospital bed and at your fiancee's funeral at the same time. Colin had been off-duty and drunk when the accident happened. Buddy didn't know how Colin would ever be able to face Marie again after what he'd done.

In ICU for weeks since he rear-ended the truck, Colin had recently been moved to a regular hospital bed but was still having his injuries monitored. Thankfully, drunk though he'd been, he had put on his seatbelt out of habit which saved his life. However, the force of the air bags deploying on contact gave him a concussion, broke his front teeth, and a number of ribs. He'd overheard one of the nurses musing about how it's always the drunk who lives after the accident and never the victim.

As bad as his physical pain was, greater still was that of realizing that no one had come to see him, not one single visitor. His parents had passed away years ago, and he hadn't kept in touch with cousins or extended family. Though he'd grown up in Halifax, he hadn't retained friendships from school days, nor had he made many friends on the force except for Buddy. If his headache hadn't been so bad, he'd examine why all that was, but not just then. All he knew was a crushing loneliness.

He thought about having a drink but then looked at his bandaged hands—chemical burns from whatever's inside the air bags. Alongside everything else, he'd been detoxed under medical supervision in the ICU. He knew he shouldn't think about drinking ever again since he was the one responsible for killing Louise. Well, the guy who kidnapped her was responsible, too, but it was Colin who had shown up hammered and driven into the back of the truck where she was lying loose. He closed his eyes, and a tear moved down one side of his face. She'd wanted to get married to him so bad, and this is what he did to her. He hadn't deserved her love, and she hadn't deserved to die.

***

Frankie's roommate called her to the front door of their apartment where, to her dismay, another police officer stood waiting.

She felt dizzy, and inhaled deeply as the anxiety app she used instructed her to do in such circumstances. Leaning one hand against the door jamb for support, she invited the officer in.

At her small kitchen table, the one Marie had given to her when she moved out, Frankie placed a glass of water beside the officer's right hand. She flicked some crumbs onto the floor while he fidgeted with his notes and clicked a pen open.

"I have some questions for you regarding the death of Cedric McCreary." Frankie didn't so much as sit down as she crumpled into the seat. Out of the corner of her eye, she could see Bea in the hallway out of sight of the police officer mouthing something frantically at her. She finally made out the words her friend was saying: LAWYER.

"Do I need a lawyer?" She asked. The officer shook his head and said, "We're just asking questions right now. You're not being charged with anything at this time." Frankie glanced at Bea who was silently waving her arms.

"I'll remain silent until I can get a lawyer," Frankie said in a voice that shook a little. Bea collapsed in relief. Putting his pen back in his chest pocket, the officer reassembled his notes and gave her an appointment to report to the police station with a lawyer. Then he took his leave. The young women gawped at each other and hugged tightly.

"Thanks, Bea. I owe you one." Frankie was shaking. "Look at my hands!" They both laughed nervously.

"Seriously, Frankie. You've got to get a good lawyer."

"How do I do that?" Frankie asked, looking blank. She felt a panic attack coming on and sat down on the floor.

***

Frankie wasn't the only one getting a visit from the authorities. Bryan Kennedy, just home from school, was surprised to see an RCMP officer sitting with his father in the living room. He took off his shoes and coat in the hallway and tried to disappear into his bedroom, but no such luck. Reluctantly, he joined them and learned the officer was there because of his Internet activity over the last several months.

In his entire life, Bryan had never wanted to bolt from a situation as much as he did this one. William placed a firm hand over his and nodded toward the RCMP officer as if to tell Bryan to stay put and cooperate. The young man's mind raced. What had he posted to get this unwanted attention? Surely, nothing so awful. He thought guiltily of his messages on Telegram. That app was secure, wasn't it? He felt the blood run from his torso to his extremities.

"First of all, I'm here to help you, son. You're still a minor. We have a warrant to go through your computer. What we've read of your messages and plans already are extremely concerning, but you haven't followed through on any of them, so there's a lot we can still do for you."

Bryan blanched while avoiding eye contact. "What's going on?"

"Your dad contacted us. Don't be mad; he did the right thing. He was rightfully concerned about the amount of time you spend online and who you're communicating with. He noticed a change in your attitude and behaviour, and gave us permission to monitor your social media posts. We found your plans to obtain materials for bomb-making and your attempts to get firearms."

William lowered his face into his palms. Bryan's eyes teared up. Few kids want to be the reason their parents make that gesture. His heart sank when his dad left the room and returned to hand the helmet and vest to the officer. Bryan's next thought was how he dreaded telling Yusra that he couldn't carry out his mission. Would he be able to tell him? Heart pounding, he only caught part of the conversation where the officer spoke about mandatory enrollment in a group for rehabilitating radicalized youth if he wanted to stay out of jail. Bryan didn't know which feelings to pay more attention to: the ones where he felt bad for letting his family down or those where his goals and approval from his online team had been thwarted.

"How bad is it?" William asked warily.

"It's serious. We have a duty to warn the family of Owen McCreary that he is or was in danger since your son made online plans to target him in his school."

William gaped at his boy. Dizzily, he wondered if he'd ever really known him. Bryan looked down at the floor, refusing to meet his gaze. For William, this was like standing at the base of a very tall mountain and trying to find a way up somehow, some way.

***

Faith's phone rang. She didn't recognize the number but picked up anyway hoping it would be Darnell.

"Hey, is this Faith?" When she confirmed it was, he went on, "I'm Bubbles, eh? Jim's brother? We call him Jim." Faith nodded even though she knew he couldn't see her.

"Are you in Labrador?" she asked.

"Yeah, he can't call you directly because the cops are out to get him, but I can call you sometimes."

"I'm just waiting for the executor to settle the estate. Then I'll have money to come out there. I hope it's done before the baby is born. That'd be easier. And tell Darnell the baby is fine."

To her annoyance, he just kind of grunted at that. "How much money are you getting? Did he tell you that I'm getting a cut of that money for helping you guys out?"

"What?" Faith was floored. Darnell most certainly had *not* told her anything of the sort.

"Yeah, Labrador is a hell of a long way from Halifax, you know. It's a freakin' nine-hour drive with a ferry and all. I did you guys a real solid. And I'm running through my savings. You could both be in jail right now if it wasn't for me."

"Right, of course." Faith said evenly, while privately fuming.

***

At the police station, Buddy called into his office a thirty-something, attractive woman. From the Philippines, maybe? Hard to say. He showed Faith into a chair across from his desk.

"We need to ask you some questions about the disappearance and death of your late husband."

"Oh, yes, certainly." She pulled a Kleenex out of her purse and blew her nose. Had she been crying? Buddy wondered, and noted a bit of an accent to her English.

"First of all, I'm sorry for your loss."

"Thank you, sir." She wiped her eyes with a carefully manicured hand. "It's hard, I miss him so much, and with the baby coming and everything." Her voice trailed off.

Buddy nodded sympathetically. "In early December, your husband, as you know, was beaten in his hospital bed. Can you tell me more about that?"

"Oh my goodness, that was awful! You trust that your husband will be safe in the hospital. What is this world coming to?"

"Yes, but did you know of any visitors to his room that may have been suspicious or anyone who'd want to hurt him?"

"Oh no, my Cedric was a good man, a city councillor, very respected. No one would want to hurt him. Why?" Then Faith wrinkled up her forehead. "Although there was a young man who came into his room the day before. Cedric told me that he was having a chat with the janitor while I was getting us coffee, when this rascal entered uninvited and threatened him. Even grabbed his sore leg! He's got diabetes, you know."

Buddy looked up sharply. "Did he say who the young man was?"

Faith shook her head. "He didn't know his name, but he was a Black kid. Do they still use that word in Canada?" She smiled weakly.

Buddy ignored the question. "Ok, what about his disappearance and murder? Did you see anyone in his room at any time who shouldn't have been there?"

Faith burst into tears, so Buddy passed a box of tissues over to her. He waited for her to calm down.

"No, I don't know what happened to my poor Cedric." She blew her nose noisily.

"All right, you're free to go."

She nodded and left the office leaving a trail of perfume behind her.

Looking over his notes, Buddy thought about the mystery maintenance man from the hospital who hadn't returned to work after Cedric disappeared. According to administration records, his name was Jim Stark and he had only worked there for a couple of months. Stark could have been Louise's abductor and the driver of the truck. There was no cell registered in that name, so he probably used a burner phone.

From interviewing a male nurse who reported he overheard a conversation between a man and a woman in a supply closet at the hospital, Buddy wondered if that had been Jim as well. According to the source, he spoke with a thick Newfoundland accent and used colorful swears native to that part of Canada. Further digging in hospital records revealed that Jim lived with his brother in a Halifax apartment. This brother, Harold Stark, had a cell phone, but couldn't be reached either, nor had he been in his apartment for several weeks. Buddy hoped that these two hadn't left the country. Finding them soon was of the utmost importance, so his next move was to get a proper warrant from a judge to authorize spyware on the brother's phone.

***

Up in Labrador City, Harold, aka Bubbles, phone rang, and he looked at the number. Faith. He picked up.

"Hey, what's up?"

"We have to be really careful," she told him. "The police interviewed me today, but I didn't tell them anything."

Bubbles exhaled loudly on the other end. "Ok, I'll only call when absolutely necessary."

"How's Darnell? Is he working at the mine yet?"

"He's ok. Not yet, but he probably will be soon. He can make good money there."

They said their goodbyes.

***

Bryan didn't talk to his dad for almost a week after the RCMP came by the house, feeling a combination of shame and anger, and he thought his dad felt the same way. The school had imposed a week of suspension, but he wasn't even off the hook for homework because his teachers sent him material. He badly wanted to send messages to his chat group to tell them about what happened, but all of his devices were under surveillance. He knew it was better than going to juvie or jail, and his dad said he should be grateful he wouldn't have a criminal record. He was, but that was hard to remember when being forced to attend youth group meetings for the radicalized. As he looked around the room at the first meeting, he saw young men who looked to be in the range of 14 to 21, some resembling what he imagined incels to look like. At least he wasn't an incel.

The RCMP officers who led the group didn't look a whole lot older than the rest of them. At each meeting, a likeable one named

Noah greeted them as they entered the room, and Bryan found himself choosing a chair closer to him. The topic of this particular meeting was spending less time online in the chat rooms that got them in trouble, and more time out in the community. Bryan started to wonder about getting back into soccer. He did miss it, and the guys, even if he would have to miss games against Owen McCreary's team because of the restraining order. He realized suddenly that playing soccer with his buddies wouldn't have been an option if the RCMP had charged him. He was beginning to count his blessings.

Early February

Released from the hospital, Colin was ordered to stay in town, in the house he used to share with Louise. It wasn't one hundred percent true that he'd had no visitors since his accident. Buddy had come by, not to see how he was so much as to rip him a new one for drinking and driving. Colin had also been visited by a representative of SIRT (Serious Incident Response Team) to tell him of charges against him for the accident and death. He hadn't healed enough to work yet, but that probably wouldn't be a problem since he'd likely lose his job. Full of self-loathing, he realized that he'd killed Louise after cheating on her, couldn't stay sober, and jeopardized his career. He hoped like hell they'd find who kidnapped Louise. Colin buried his face in his hands and wept.

***

Colin woke up hung over and wanted to skip his mandatory Alcoholic Anonymous meeting, a condition of his DUI charges, but he knew he had to report to an officer, so he made himself go.

He chose a meeting he could get to on his bus route since he'd totalled his car and lost his license. Not being able to drive was a real loss. As he placed his coat on the back of a chair in the church basement, he looked around the room. There were tables set up at the front with various booklets presided over by two men and two women. People were placing chairs in a semi-circle while others were getting themselves a cup of coffee.

"Are you new here?" A sweet-looking older woman asked Colin.

"Yes." He didn't like how interactive this was already shaping up to be. Colin wanted to just show up as mandated and leave without actually talking to anyone.

The meeting opened and people were invited to share. Colin didn't want to, but the peer pressure and the structured format almost demanded it.

"I'm Colin and I'm an alcoholic." He was mortified to find his voice break on the last word.

"Hi, Colin." Everyone spoke in unison.

"I haven't had a drink today." Though he meant it as a shameful admission that he had indeed drunk yesterday, Colin was surprised that people nodded in encouragement.

He stayed behind after the meeting to stack the chairs and clean the coffee area. He was rinsing the coffee pot when he felt someone tap him on the back. It was Marie, Louise's mother, and he felt his heart pound, sure that she must hate him, not that he could blame her.

"Marie," he whispered.

"Colin," she said simply.

"I'm *so* sorry, Marie." He looked like he was blinking back tears. "I am just so sorry." Colin was not a bad man, but he wasn't a good man either, Marie thought. She remembered that he could be kind at times, had been competent at his job when not drunk, and that her dear Louise had loved him.

"I was so angry with you before, Colin. That's why you haven't heard from me until now."

Colin nodded vigorously, afraid to talk.

"But I've known for a while that you're an alcoholic."

Colin looked at her surprised. "How'd you know?"

"Because it takes one to know one." She answered.

"You?" Colin gaped at her. She nodded.

"Do you remember that time you couldn't find your vodka bottle in the cooking pot in the closet at your house?" Colin certainly did remember that. He'd been puzzled as fuck as to where it had gone. Made no sense. He'd not suspected Marie was onto him.

"I've been attending AA for decades. I'm glad you're coming. It'll do you good."

"Marie, I wouldn't blame you for hating me."

"Oh, get over yourself, Colin. I don't have the energy for hate. Life's hard enough. If you want to honour Louise and make it up, quit drinking for God's sake." She patted him on the back and left. He stood there until he realized he was still holding the coffee pot.

***

David and his family were chatting and watching the news just before dinner at William's house when the screen caught David's attention.

"Look!" He walked up to the TV and stood right in front of it.

"Please move to the side, dear," Ruth asked.

As the announcer told of the charging of Frankie Gabriel, the janitor at the hospital, in the beating of Cedric McCreary in December, Bryan looked over at his father who had turned an ominous shade of grey as if all the blood had drained from his face. Looking at his grandfather, Bryan caught the older man also staring at William. Bryan did not like the look on his grandfather's face. Not one little bit.

David, visibly shaken by the news, went into his bedroom and stared at his own face in the mirror over the dresser. William had reacted strongly to the news that the young woman custodian was arrested for the beating. Had he done it?

David returned to see Bryan sitting as if frozen in his seat. William excused himself to the bathroom, and Ruth looked at her grandson, asking gently, "What's wrong, Bryan?"

"I think Dad did it." Bryan whispered. His grandparents' eyes widened in disbelief. He went on. "That day Dad said he got blisters from shoveling without gloves, but our shovel was broken. Neither of us shoveled anything. Why'd he lie?"

William came out of the bathroom to find everyone staring at him.

"William, tell me the truth. Did you beat that old man?" David asked. Ruth and Bryan waited in silence for the answer, but William stubbornly refused to talk about it.

"We're leaving," William said firmly to Bryan who looked bewildered.

"If you don't tell me, I will have to tell the police what I suspect," David said solemnly.

"Are you sure?" Ruth asked him quietly.

He nodded. William put on his coat and shoes, and Bryan looked apologetically back at his grandparents as they left.

"What about dinner, Dad?" Bryan asked in the car. "I'm hungry."

"We'll go to McDonald's."

Dad never eats at McDonald's, so things must be really bad, thought Bryan.

***

Frankie's roommate had insisted that Frankie see a doctor about her mental state. Bea even went to the appointment at the walk-in clinic with her because she knew her friend trusted the medical establishment only marginally more than the justice system. Frankie came away with a prescription for an antidepressant which was thankfully covered by her benefits. Maybe this would help with her grief about Louise and the chronic lack of sleep.

In court, Frankie and her lawyer sat in the front row and Marie sat primly directly behind them. Every once in a while Frankie looked back at her and Marie would nod supportively. She noticed Bryan Kennedy sitting in the courtroom beside his family members. Although she hadn't known his name, she'd remember him anywhere. He'd stood up to that old, racist bastard for her. She wondered if the teenager had beat Cedric?

The first evidence presented by the prosecution when Frankie took the stand was the pair of work gloves and the broom which had dark brown stains along the handle making Frankie feel ill.

Her defence lawyer rebutted. "This is circumstantial evidence at best. Even though you have video footage of Ms. Gabriel in the supply room, she'd have to enter there regularly simply to get the tools to do her job. She's also not the only person with access to that supply room. Anyone with a pass card could get in or prop the door open as someone else leaves. "

The next piece of evidence was a beaded ornament.

"Can you tell me what this is?" The prosecution asked Frankie on the stand. Mortified, Frankie gaped at her lawyer who nodded encouragement.

"It's a medicine wheel that I beaded. I put it on the Christmas tree in the hospital hallway on my floor. When I took down the tree, I noticed it was missing.

"That's because it was found in the bag with Cedric's body in the bog." The prosecution answered.

Frankie stared at her hands which were shaking while her lawyer looked unconcerned.

As a rebuttal, he said, "Frankie has not been charged with the death of Cedric McCreary, so the presence of this beaded ornament in the bag where his body was found is irrelevant. It was likely put there in an attempt to misdirect the murder investigation away from the real culprit and toward my client, who is innocent of all charges."

Next, the defence showed the court grainy footage of the hallway near Room 22 and storage room from the night of the beating. It showed a stocky Black man getting a broom and gloves.

"Objection, your honor. The prosecution wasn't told of this footage."

"May I explain, your honor?"

The judge nodded.

"There were problems with the video cameras in the supply closet, so I've been working with an IT specialist to get this footage back, and we just obtained it. It's not perfect, but you can clearly see someone else in there that night."

"I'll allow it." The judge agreed.

Bryan looked at his father, who had gone an unhealthy shade of grey. Suddenly, the young man stood up from the audience. "Excuse me, your honour." He addressed the judge who raised his eyebrows. "May I speak?"

The judge allowed it despite the objections of both lawyers, and the court hummed audibly when he clearly said, "It was me. I beat the old man. One day I overheard how rude he was being to the janitor lady. I'm so sick of people's racism, I had to defend her, but I admit that I went too far."

"But how..." The judge trailed off.

"The night after he was so awful to her, I vowed revenge for her, for everyone who gets treated badly, so I sneaked into the supply room and got the gloves and broom. Then when no one was in the hallway, I entered his room and hit him." He lowered his head.

Next, the prosecution responded to Bryan's claim. "Young man, I sincerely doubt that it was you, and I'm not sure why you would lie about this in court. May I remind you that perjury is a felony and punishable by law? If it was you, what did you do with the broom and gloves?"

Bryan stammered, "Uh, I... uh, put them back in the storage room."

The prosecutor shook his head. "Wrong. They were found in the dumpster behind the hospital."

"That'll do, young man, you may be seated. I'll deal with you later." After calming the crowd in the courtroom, the judge called the prosecution and defence up to the front.

"Who is this on the video?" The prosecutor asked testily.

"I believe it's the perpetrator, your honor. He's in the courtroom. Permission to call him to the stand?" The judge agreed to the defence's request.

William was called up and sat himself down glumly.

"Is that you in the video?"

"Yes," William answered. Sure enough, his appearance matched right down to his gait.

"This footage was reclaimed as well," the defence lawyer said, showing video sometimes pixelated of the same man in the back of the hospital tossing a broom and gloves into a dumpster.

On cross examination, the prosecutor asked, "So, Mr. Kennedy, you belatedly say you committed the crime, but the footage isn't very clear. Are you just trying to cover for Ms Gabriel? Is this some kind of gallant gesture?"

"Objection, your honour." The defence interjected. "Mr Kennedy is currently wearing the same cardigan sweater that he's wearing in the video." He pointed to the screen which had frozen the image, and sure enough, despite the poor video quality, it was the same.

The prosecution sat down and the defence attorney asked William why he did it.

"What I'm going to say doesn't sound like a good enough reason to beat an old man, but he was just so horrible." William sighed. "All my life I've heard the stories of the unfairness that went on in our community of Africville, and we've lived it, too, here in Halifax. Do you know we're known as the Alabama of the North?"

When no one answered, he continued. "Our community has experienced such overt and covert racism, and I've always tried to fight it the peaceful way. I've been on city committees, volunteered for groups to promote good relations, and prayed about it, but it's never fixed the problem. It's the most frustrating thing in the world, and it just won't get better. My father suffered because of Cedric McCreary years ago, and after all these generations, my son is still taking abuse from his grandson. It's intolerable. I couldn't take it anymore."

The court, lawyers, and judge were silent. You could have heard the proverbial pin drop.

"I don't know why my son confessed to something he didn't do. He's young and misguided right now. Please don't hold it against him." William bowed his head and a tear dropped onto his thigh.

Frankie, her lawyer, and Marie hugged when the judge dropped the charges of aggravated assault. Frankie wept from relief and Marie held her as she had so many times when she was a lost little girl.

"So it wasn't the boy who came to my rescue who did it," she said to her lawyer who hugged her again. "I'm glad about that."

The judge took Bryan and William into his chambers along with the bailiff. Bryan was smartly scolded for lying in court, but let off with increased community service. William, however, was to appear in court again on charges of aggravated assault to which he would plead guilty.

At home, William tried to tell Bryan the importance of always being honest, but it didn't go over well.

"Yeah, you too, Dad." He said sarcastically.

"Why did you say you did it?" William asked his son.

"Because I was covering for you!" Bryan started to cry.

His dad hugged him tight and whispered, "Thanks, Bryan, but you don't have to do that for me.

Chapter Eight

Mid-February

The upshot of Colin's court trial was that he was sentenced to a minimum of eight years in prison. He accepted his fate, knowing full-well he shouldn't have been driving and was responsible for the death of his fianceé. There was never any doubt about that. In the past, the province had been accused of being too lenient with police officers who committed crimes, so unfortunately for Colin, the justice system was now clamping down. Bad luck for him.

Marie visited him from time to time, and he continued to attend AA meetings in prison.

"How's it going in there?" Marie asked, aware of the guard standing near their table.

"Well, it's prison. Not easy being a cop in here, you know?"

Marie just nodded, as though she did. "Does anyone else visit you besides me?"

Colin shook his head. Marie thought about the nice police officer that had been at their engagement party in the fall. "What was that man's name?"

"Buddy," Colin replied. "I think he hates me now."

***

On Valentine's Day, Marie who had been sober for 25 years, found herself wanting a drink. Instead of giving in to the impulse, she went to a meeting and was glad to see Colin there; she hadn't been sure he was committed to his sobriety. His eyes were red-rimmed because today was to have been his and Louise's wedding day, but instead of a wedding, they'd had a funeral. There would be no kids for Colin and Louise and no grandchildren for Marie. For both of them, it was a difficult anniversary.

***

Up in Labrador City, Darnell's eye was getting worse. It felt like it still had traces of the bog mud that got into it when he was dumping Cedric McCreary's body. Afraid of authorities, he hadn't seen a doctor, preferring to use over-the-counter eye drops from the pharmacy. As far as he could tell, they weren't doing jack-shit.

He wanted to call Faith himself instead of relying on his brother for that, but you needed ID to get a prepaid calling card, and he didn't want to do anything to call attention to himself. He was a cash-only guy for the time being. He got Bubbles to call her on his phone, and then he took over.

"Babe?"

"Oh, thank God, Darnell. How are you doing?" Faith lowered her voice even though she was alone.

"Not great. I miss you, baby. And my eye's fucked. I got something in it. I think it's infected."

"Oh no. Did you go to the doctor?"

"Can't, babe. I have to lay low."

"Oh yeah, right. Are you working yet?"

Darnell felt some irritation. "Not yet 'cause of the eye. Soon though, when it's better. When you coming out here?"

"Not sure yet. Still waiting to hear about the will."

"Hmmm. How's our baby?" Darnell perked up thinking about that. He hoped for a boy, a junior. He planned to be a better dad than his horrible old man had been. That shouldn't be hard.

Faith smiled. "Great, our baby's great, but if the money doesn't come through in time, I may be having the baby here in June. I can get my mom to help me for a bit after and then come to Labrador. What's it like there? "

"It's cold, hon, but so is Halifax. Hey, I want you both out here with me as soon as you can."

"I know, sweetie. I'm trying."

When she hung up, Faith felt frustrated because the will was taking so long to get sorted out and because Darnell wasn't working yet. Was he actually even going to be able to be a good provider for her and the baby? Her mother always said a woman needed that most of all, and she'd been very disappointed when her lawyer told her that she would get none of Cedric's money if she was found guilty.

Darnell also felt frustrated with Faith. Why wouldn't she come to Labrador sooner? Surely the money coming to them didn't depend on her staying in Halifax. Was she planning to join him at all, or was he losing her? He vaped and tried to forget about it.

***

Buddy and a fellow officer went over the results of the recent search.

"That woman seemed pretty upset that we had a warrant," Buddy's colleague said, cataloguing the items they took from her home.

"Yes, Faith Santos. It's a big case. We're getting close to charging her with murder in the death of her husband. No wonder she freaked out."

"Especially when we confiscated her phone."

"It's okay. She'll get it back—after we get court permission to put spyware on it."

***

In mid-February, Faith was charged with the murder of her husband, Cedric McCreary and assigned a lawyer by the court. When her court date arrived, the judge asked how she was pleading.

"Not guilty," the lawyer answered. Faith, dressed in a modest navy blue dress suit, sat beside him looking morose. Buddy, who sat in the back of the courtroom, figured her lawyer must have instructed her how to dress because every time he'd ever seen Faith, she had been wearing flamboyant clothing. Frankie slipped into the row behind Buddy just as the proceedings were starting.

When Faith was called to the stand, she looked down demurely, and it occurred to Buddy that she might be a pretty good actor.

"Tell us in your own words what you know of your husband's death." The judge instructed.

Somewhat theatrically, in Buddy's opinion, she wiped a tear away from her cheek with a tissue.

"On the night he disappeared, I tucked him in for the night and kissed him. I didn't know I'd never see him alive again." She blew her nose. "When I heard the next morning that he was gone, I didn't know what to think. It didn't make any sense, and it took nearly a month for the police to find his body." She choked back a sob.

On cross-examination, the prosecutor asked Faith, "Who have you been getting phone calls from?"

Faith's mouth fell open. "Excuse me?"

"There are calls you've received from Labrador City. Who is calling you?"

"Uh, a friend."

"Is it an accomplice?"

"No, no, of course not. He's just a friend."

Buddy thought that Faith's usual composure had failed her this time as she had just lied on the stand, and her lawyer's face went pale. Buddy knew about these calls since the spyware on Faith's phone had led to him getting court permission to install it on Bubbles' phone as well. First, the cell site simulator had tricked the burner phone into revealing his location, then the dumbass had fallen for clicking on their link on social media, which opened up conversations between Faith and Darnell, the boyfriend. Turns out the dumbass was Darnell's brother who must have helped Darnell get out of Halifax after Louise's abduction.

Next, the coroner took the stand, and the courtroom hushed.

"The cause of death for Cedric McCreary was strangulation."

Faith heaved a sigh of relief. There was no way anyone would think she, in her pregnant state, would be capable of strangling anyone, never mind disposing of a body. She glanced hopefully at her lawyer who didn't seem very relieved and she wondered what he was thinking.

The prosecutor asked the coroner, "What else did you find?"

"There was evidence of tetrahydrozoline poisoning." The crowd muttered excitedly.

"Please explain for the court what that is."

"Tetrahydrozoline is a drug found in eye drops. If ingested, it can lead to multiple organ damage. Mr. McCreary's blood and urine tests showed the presence of this drug. Most likely he ingested up to 60 millilitres of the fluid over several days. It would not have any taste if put into food or drink."

Frankie thought back to the times she'd cleaned Cedric's room. On his tray were the usual assortment of items that patients often have: tissues, lip balm, and yes, eye drops. Too bad Louise wasn't alive to testify; she'd know exactly what Cedric had used.

The coroner continued. "Symptoms he had in the hospital before his disappearance were bradycardia..."

"Which is?" The judge prompted.

"Slow heart rate and also a reduction in alertness."

"But that's not what killed him?"

"No, he died of strangulation."

"Would the tetrahydrozoline have killed him?"

"In enough quantity and over time, yes."

The defence attorney posited that Faith, being pregnant, was unable to strangle and dispose of a body. The prosecution suggested she had motive, being a beneficiary to Cedric upon his death.

"But they were already married, so she had a nice lifestyle. She's even expecting a baby. She had no reason to want him dead," the defence argued.

Buddy thought she couldn't have been acting alone. No way could she have moved that body by herself. She must have had an accomplice, that Jim/Darnell. Get her old rich husband out of the picture, and they could split his money.

Next, the nurse who had talked to the police about what he'd heard outside the supply closet was called to the stand by the prosecutor. Once sworn in, he spoke of overhearing a man and woman discussing moving someone. He also recalled the man saying he needed to do something about a female nurse.

When the defence lawyer argued that the witness hadn't actually seen who was in the closet, the man mentioned what he referred to as a "Newfie" accent.

The defence attorney snorted. "That's circumstantial at best."

Faith sat fidgeting in her seat as video footage showed the court images of her and Darnell in the supply room.

She whispered to her lawyer, "I thought hospitals weren't allowed to have cameras."

Her lawyer sighed, "They can't in the patients' rooms, but they can in hallways and closets. I told you before to be honest with me. I can't help you if I don't know the whole truth. Who *is* that anyway?"

Faith refused to answer.

When the court session ended, Frankie tugged on Buddy's sleeve.

"Buddy, I heard at work that the McCreary family is suing the hospital for negligence."

Buddy raised his eyebrows.

"Do you think they'll get anywhere with it?" She asked.

"Tough to say. It doesn't look good on the hospital that it happened on their watch, but the burden is on the prosecution to prove negligence beyond a reasonable doubt, and I'm not sure they can do that."

She looked around and lowered her voice. "Do you think I need to worry about being charged with anything again?"

He put his hand on her shoulder and answered, "I don't think so, Frankie. You were found not guilty of the beating, and it looks more and more like Faith might have had a hand in his death."

She looked at the floor and nodded. With a quick, small smile she looked up and said, "I have some information you might be interested in. Do you have time to talk?"

He said that he did, so they walked to a nearby coffee shop.

Once they ordered and found a table in the corner away from other patrons, Frankie told him about a cousin of hers who lives in Labrador City.

"My cousin, Trey works at the grocery store there and he notices when new people come to town. There's this guy Trey says reminds him of one of the guys from The Trailer Park Boys, you know that show?"

Buddy snickered, "Yes, I do. Which of the Trailer Park Boys does this guy look like?"

"The one with the Coke-bottle glasses."

"Bubbles."

Frankie nodded. "Anyway, this Bubbles came into the grocery store awhile ago with a guy with a messed-up eye. No one's seen him around since, but word around town is that Bubbles is buying lots of painkillers on the street, but doesn't seem to be the one using them. Rumour has it that something's majorly wrong with the sick guy."

"Well, I don't want that bastard dying before we can put him away. He and his brother need to do jail time."

Buddy thanked Frankie and got Trey's contact information and made plans to contact the Royal Newfoundland Constabulary in Labrador to follow up as soon as possible .

***

Bryan showered after his indoor soccer practice and made himself a large sandwich. William put his hand on his shoulder. "I need to talk to you."

"Can I eat while you talk?"

William nodded, and they sat at the kitchen table. "I've apologized to Grandpa and Grandma for the beating, and for lying to everyone about it. They've forgiven me, thank God, but I've disappointed them very much."

Bryan felt relieved to hear that.

His father continued, "Also, I had my court appearance and they charged me with aggravated assault. I pleaded guilty because I am guilty, and now I have a Conditional Sentence Order."

Bryan looked blankly at his father.

"It's called house arrest. It means I don't have to serve prison time, but I have conditions for two years. I have to report to a probation officer, obey a curfew, and stay away from Cedric McCreary's relatives. If I don't, I'll be arrested."

Bryan was uncharacteristically speechless. He chewed his food thoughtfully then said, "How did you manage no jail time?"

William sighed. "It's because I had no prior record, I'm not part of a terrorist or criminal organization, and I'm not considered to be a danger to the public. Although if I ever did anything like this again, I'd be hooped."

David's eyes widened and then he smiled. "You're as bad as me with my online bullshit, but it's also kind of badass, Dad."

"Seriously, Bryan, don't make me into a hero," William said sternly. "What I did was wrong. I've spent most of my life trying to get justice for our people by the book, but in the end I couldn't meet my own high standards and ended up beating an elderly man. Maybe I glorified the idea of Grandpa punching Cedric back in the day, and I wanted to be a hero like that, too. No, Bryan. I'm not a bad ass, maybe just an ass.""

Bryan laughed, and then William admitted that he was embarrassed to show up at church these days or to look his own parents in their eyes, and they both laughed. Sometimes, William thought, when you've done a lot of crying, all you can do *is* laugh.

Chapter Nine

March

At his weekly youth meeting, Bryan admitted to Noah that before the police had shut down his access, he'd tried to communicate with his online chat group, but they'd largely ghosted him.

"Yeah, that's what they always do. They are not your friends, Bryan. They pretend to be your friend to get you to commit their crimes, but they ditch you as soon as you get caught or refuse to do their bidding."

Bryan decided to sign up for cleaning up garbage on the roadside as his community service obligations. There were other tasks he could've chosen, but he liked the idea of working independently but with other youth nearby doing the same thing. His dad had been surprised that's what his son had chosen, but Bryan found it oddly rewarding. He liked everything about it from wearing a florescent vest, to seeing the garbage bag fill up with each item big or small. After several bags, the roadside really did look better. Sure, you found some disgusting things sometimes—carcasses, used condoms, and drug paraphernalia, but overall, it felt good to clean.

"Now for your room," his dad joked. "Hardee har har."

***

Faith used a burner phone and left a message for Bubbles. It took a couple of hours before he called her back.

"I went out to get some pain killers for your boyfriend. He's not doing so good."

"Is it still his eye?" Faith asked impatiently.

"Yeah, it's real bad. Got some bog shit in there when he dropped the body. He's sleeping right now, or I'd put him on."

Faith was going to ask if Darnell had gotten a job yet, but the question seemed moot. Instead she filled Bubbles in on what had happened in court, and that it wasn't looking good for them since the authorities now knew of Darnell's existence.

"Well, fuck me." Bubbles knew then that he'd have to ditch his burner phone.

***

That night, Faith considered her options carefully. By now, the court obviously knew that Darnell was her lover. She put her hands on her growing belly. She was over five months along now and could feel the light butterfly-like movements of the baby. It had been a few months since she'd even seen Darnell, and it sounded like he was in a weakened state and not improving. How could she possibly depend on him to take care of her and the baby? She didn't want to go all the way to Labrador City and end up taking care of *him*.

Her decision to give up on Darnell emerged less like a light bulb turning on and more like a dimmer switch being slowly turned up. It was as clear as a bell to her now that she needed to switch tactics in light of changing circumstances. To cling to the original plan with

Darnell would shackle her and the baby to a losing proposition. This way, she'd get to keep Cedric's money all for herself. On to Plan B.

***

Buddy was called to the stand in court to testify as to what was found in Faith's apartment and in Cedric's hospital room.

"First of all, the empty bottle of eye drops at the hospital had no fingerprints on it. Someone had wiped it clean." He stated.

"Objection. Drawing conclusions." Faith's lawyer said to the judge.

"Sustained. Please refrain from drawing conclusions."

"That's only circumstantial evidence anyway," Faith's lawyer whispered to her.

"Secondly, we located a receipt in the garbage at her home for three bottles of eye drops at 30 mL each."

"A lot of people use eye drops." Faith muttered to her lawyer.

Buddy continued, "The receipt had been shredded using a shredder found onsite, but we were able to piece it back together." There was a murmur in the courtroom. The judge tapped his gavel for order.

"Finally, on her laptop's history, we found searches related to tetrahydrozoline poisoning." The courtroom gave a unified gasp. Faith's lawyer wouldn't meet her nervous gaze.

"We'd monitored her calls and there is one she received from an unknown number where she spoke to a man." Buddy began to read from a script. "We have to be really careful. The police interviewed me today, but I didn't tell them anything. Ok, I'll only call if absolutely necessary."

He waited for the noise in the court to die down again. Buddy continued to read, "How's Darnell? Is he working yet?' The man answered, 'He's ok. Not working yet, but he can probably get a job in the mine. It's good money.'"

Faith looked down at the table top; her lawyer was fidgeting in the chair beside her. The judge sat back in his chair.

"Where is this Darnell?" He asked.

"I don't know." Faith replied.

"May I request a recess?" The defence lawyer asked.

A meeting with the judge, prosecutor, and defence lawyer resulted in a change in the charge against Faith from first degree murder to attempted murder. What her lawyer had finally gotten out of Faith was that she and Darnell were indeed lovers and that they planned to "help Cedric pass away quicker because he was suffering and *dying anyway.*" She hadn't counted on Darnell deciding to dispose of the body without telling her, nor for Cedric to be still alive at the bog which lead to Darnell strangling him. It wasn't a good look for a woman to attempt to poison her husband so she and her beau could run away with the money, but there you had it. If convicted of attempted murder, Faith could be looking at anywhere from four to seven years or as much as life in prison—baby or no baby.

Faith's lawyer had often wondered at her overconfidence about the outcome of this trial. Maybe she'd been in denial about how much jail time she could end up serving. Or perhaps she thought she'd get off scot-free.

"Even though the charge has been downgraded to attempted murder instead of first degree murder, it's not really a benefit to you, Faith. All it shows is that you seriously meant to kill your husband. The fact that you didn't succeed doesn't matter. You can't even argue it was impulsive." At this, he felt annoyed that Faith actually pouted.

***

Faith got off the phone after talking to her lawyer about her late husband's estate. If she was found guilty of attempted murder, there would be no money coming her way. None at all. Her chest felt tight when she considered that she had a baby on the way and no income. For the first time, it occurred to her that perhaps it hadn't been such a good idea to kill Cedric, that this whole plan with Darnell depended on them getting away with it. Obviously, a life with Darnell was no longer an option. He was going down for murder for sure.

She cried into her pillow for a while and then looked into the mirror in her bedroom. She used make-up remover to take off what remained of her mascara, patted her round belly, and breathed deeply.

"Don't worry, little one. We're going to land on our feet." With that, she scrolled through her old texts until she found one from the autumn, a guy she'd hooked up with a few times through an app. She contacted her lawyer with his contact information. Time to let him know he's going to be a daddy.

***

From inside prison, Colin had been following the news of the trial and getting updates from Marie who attended most of the court dates.

"I talked to Buddy about him coming to visit you sometime." The older woman said.

Colin hardly dared to get his hopes up. "And what did he say?"

"Well, he's very angry at you for what you did, but I told him that holding a grudge doesn't make the world a better place, and I do believe he's a man who dearly wants to make this world a better place."

"Thanks, Marie. It's more than I deserve."

She smiled wryly. "You got that right. Anyway, he's thinking about it. I told him if I can forgive you then so can he."

Colin nodded. He was surprised to see Buddy at one of the open AA meetings the following week. He gingerly approached his former friend afterwards.

"Hey, Buddy."

The police officer dressed in civilian clothes for this event, police officers not being popular among inmates and all. "Hey." The two men looked awkwardly at each other for a few minutes, and then Buddy clapped Colin on the shoulder.

"How you doing in here?" He asked. Colin smiled in relief and told him he was as good as could be expected but that he'd been contacted by someone recently and thought he should tell somebody in law enforcement.

They pulled a couple of chairs together in the corner and spoke quietly. Buddy listened as Colin told him of the unexpected call he got.

"It was from Faith's lawyer saying I'm the father of her child." Buddy looked at him, wide-eyed.

"So you and she…?"

Colin nodded. "I know. I'm a shithead, and yes, the timing of the pregnancy tracks. Last fall I got together with her a few times, and then we faded out. I never expected to hear from her again." He said glumly.

"Ever hear of birth control?" Buddy muttered, annoyed.

"She said she was on the pill," Colin said lamely.

Buddy shook his head. "Wow, bro."

"Anyway, I told her we're getting a paternity test done asap."

"Yeah, man. You need to know if it's really yours before you can decide anything else."

Colin nodded. "Hey, do you ever see Frankie? I feel so bad about what happened with Louise." He paused for a moment to collect himself.

"Yeah, she comes to Faith's trial when she's not working, but she hasn't said too much about you. I think it rocked her world that she had to go to court about the old man's beating."

"And then I killed her best friend," Colin wiped at his eyes with the sleeve of his prison uniform. Buddy didn't answer.

***

The search parameters on Darnell Smith by the Royal Newfoundland Constabulary and the Halifax police revealed a man with several aliases. So far, no one had found him or the man called Bubbles although they were suspected to still be in or near Labrador City. Neither had anyone matching the description of the former hospital maintenance man applied for a job at the mine. Darnell's phone had been located in a wooded area prompting officers to believe that he'd suspected the spyware and gotten rid of it.

Languishing on an old mattress on the floor of a slumlord's basement was where a very unhealthy Darnell lay. For the most part, he was alone. Sometimes his brother brought him food and any drugs he could find, which helped with the pain for a bit until they wore off, but Bubbles wasn't home much because he was out selling drugs. By this time, the eye infection had spread to the other eye and over the whole upper part of his face. Darnell slipped in and out of consciousness.

***

In Halifax, the court began a separate trial for Darnell to try him in absentia for murder. Faith's lawyer wasn't sure yet whether he'd be charged with multiple offences including attempted murder or first degree murder.

Faith didn't tell her lawyer that she no longer cared what happened to Darnell, that she'd moved on from him. Instead, she asked who was being called to testify today.

Turns out it was Colin Doughty who had been subpoenaed to provide evidence of Faith's dishonesty. Faith was unpleasantly surprised to see him in prison garb. Although she'd heard that he had been convicted of DUI manslaughter, she hadn't really processed that he was currently doing time. She briefly wondered if she'd be able to get money out of him, but then she remembered that he must have a pension that they couldn't take away from him. She'd benefit from that, too.

While the judge got organized, Colin looked at the people crowded into the courtroom. He recognized quite a few familiar faces: Frankie, Buddy, Marie, and the Kennedys including the grandson who must have taken the morning off school to be there. The young man's dad wasn't there, but the McCreary family was.

The prosecutor asked Colin to tell the court about his relationship with Faith. He'd spoken with a lawyer at length in preparation for this court appearance. Their affair was a loaded topic for so many people in the audience, and Colin knew that his actions had caused a great deal of pain.

"I met her in the fall of last year at a coffee shop. We found each other on an app. We met a few times at a hotel." Several attendees gasped in unison.

The defence asked on cross examination, "Did you know that Faith was already married?"

"No, I didn't."

"Did you ask?" The defence asked abruptly.

Colin looked down and shook his head.

"Say it out loud for the court."

"No, I didn't ask her if she was married." He avoided looking at anyone he knew in the room.

"Why did you discontinue the relationship with the defendant?"

"Well, it just fizzled out. We saw each other a few times for sex, that was it. But..." He stopped.

"Continue, please."

"The baby is mine."

Everyone gasped. Not wanting to, Colin forced himself to look at the audience. Frankie and Marie sat there with their mouths hanging open, Buddy stared straight ahead like a concrete statue, his lips a straight line, and Cedric's family was in a total uproar.

When the judge quieted the courtroom, Colin said, "We did a paternity test. The baby is mine."

After Colin was excused, the prosecutor called up Faith. She held her head high refusing to accept any shame. Colin envied her.

"Well, at first I thought the baby was Darnell's." Faith began.

"You didn't think it was your husband's?" The prosecutor asked.

"Of course not." Faith said haughtily. There were disgusted murmurs from Cedric's family members.

"How can you be so sure? Were you not sexual with your husband?"

Faith said, "I performed my wifely duties when I had to, but Cedric was impotent. Everyone knows his son is adopted. Cedric has never fathered children, not even when he was young."

While this *was* factually correct, the way she said it made Cedric's son stand up and shout, "Hey!"

"Please be seated," the judge instructed. To the prosecutor he said, "continue."

The courtroom seemed to hold its breath as the prosecutor prompted her for more information.

"Colin Doughty has testified that a paternity test confirms him as the child's father." She confirmed, almost proudly.

Colin was aware of the gravity of his situation, and right now he felt absolutely overwhelmed. How would all of this play out? He had no idea.

Chapter Ten

April

Marie sat in the half-dark in a confessional at her church.

"Forgive me, Father, for I have sinned." The priest listened calmly to her list of mostly petty transgressions, but perked up when she told of her anger towards Colin. She had tried to forgive him, but what she'd heard about him getting Faith pregnant while being engaged to Louise was beyond her abilities.

"I feel for the first time that I hate someone." She confessed. The priest, one she'd known for decades, listened carefully before answering.

"This is the true test of God's love. Hate can be the easiest response to hurt, may even seem justified, and we can get stuck there in our righteous anger, but God calls on us to forgive, not just for the sake of the sinner, but for our own sake and that of other people we care about."

Marie went home and cried, but she did take to heart what he had said.

***

"Should I even play against his team next week?" Bryan asked his dad. His soccer team was scheduled to play Owen McCreary's.

"I don't know. You'd better check with Noah to see if you're even allowed to. And I can't come to watch that game since I have to stay away from anyone named McCreary."

It occurred to Bryan that Noah from the youth rehab group had replaced his online connections as someone he looked to for guidance. Noah was someone he could visit and talk to in person, not just through a computer. He also noticed that Noah never required anything in particular of Bryan. He no longer felt that he had to do bad things to prove himself.

***

After Colin's confession, Frankie felt like someone had punched her in the solar plexus. Louise wasn't here to live through this and that was a small mercy, but Frankie took on what would have been her late friend's pain as though it were her own and it had been consuming her for days. She desperately needed to talk to someone, but who? She would have phoned Marie, but she must be in her own pain. Bea was on holiday out west.

Court had adjourned and she didn't know when it would reconvene. It was her day off and she didn't work tomorrow until late afternoon, so she decided to drive out to the rez to visit her father.

"Hey, Frankie," Ujjl greeted her with a pat on the back. Not generally good with people's feelings, his face clouded over when he saw her red-rimmed eyes.

"Can I have a hug, Dad?" In answer, he enveloped her in a big bear hug. It occurred to her they had never been a hugging family, but that they should start.

He offered her a cup of tea, and they sat at his tired kitchen table.

"How're you doing, Dad? Any more seizures?"

"So far, so good." Ujjl answered. His diabetes had contributed to him developing epilepsy, but it was being controlled by the medication he'd gotten several months ago.

Frankie sighed. "I want to say again how sorry I am that I didn't go to the hospital with you and Louise that time. I was really freaked out by the police asking to see me. Bad memories, you know?"

Her dad smiled. "It's ok, Frankie. I know."

"No, I should have been there. I still feel awful about it."

"And we still haven't talked about you running off into the woods by yourself," he gently scolded. "You scared the bejesus out of me and Joan. You could've died if we hadn't found you in time."

Frankie started to cry. "I'm so sorry, Dad. I just couldn't handle the thought of being hauled in by the police and questioned. Maybe they'd blame me or make up something. I just don't trust them."

"I've had my run-ins with cops in my time, too, but they aren't all bad. That guy Buddy seems okay."

Frankie nodded, then filled him in on the events of Faith's trial over the past months. Because her father had always seemed disinterested in the details of her life, she'd long ago stopped telling him about them, but she wanted a different kind of relationship with him now, a better one. At times weeping, Frankie spared no details.

"Holy shit," he responded. "But why didn't you tell me about your charges?"

"Because I didn't want you to worry."

"You should tell me that stuff, Frankie. I know I wasn't there for you growing up, but I can be there now." His eyes watered and he put his hand over hers. Frankie looked down at his veiny hand, warm and dry. She agreed to keep him up to date on what was going on with Faith's trial and the baby that Colin had fathered. She realized she'd once harboured hopes of being an aunty to Louise's children, even if not biologically, but that dream had died with her best friend.

"Maybe you can be an aunty to Colin's child anyway," Ujjl suggested quietly.

"What?" Frankie started. "I don't think so. Deal with that bitch, Faith? I meant to tell Louise about her and Colin back in December but she died before I got up the courage."

"Maybe it's just as well. Anyway, I heard it takes a village to raise a child," Ujjl said, patting her hand. "That kid's gonna need a lot of help."

***

In Labrador City, a passerby noticed a heap of clothing on the sidewalk outside the emergency department of the regional hospital. Inside of that heap was the man known as Darnell. How did he get there? Well, eventually the drugs Bubbles brought to him couldn't keep the pain at bay, nor could they cure his blood infection which resulted from orbital cellulitis. Bacteria from bog mud in his eye had spread through his bloodstream, and he was close to death. His brother, not knowing what else to do, dropped Darnell at the curb and fled.

Chapter Eleven

July

In the end, it was the police phone recordings that provided the conclusive evidence to put Faith away, aided by the shredded eye drops receipt and the testimony of the male nurse. Although pregnant, Faith's sentence meant serving a minimum of four years at the Nova Institution for Women in Truro. The baby would live with her in prison.

***

In the prison visiting room with Colin, Marie's thin fingers worked on her knitting project, a yellow baby blanket.

"I mean Faith *does* deserve to go to prison, but what about the baby? Is that any place to raise a kid?" He asked wearily.

"It is what it is, Colin. I always hated that expression, but it fits here." Marie answered. "It's better to keep the child with its mother, and maybe Faith'll get out earlier if she behaves herself. You too."

"Yeah, I guess. At least I'll be allowed supervised visits once the baby's born."

"By the way, did that nasty McCreary family get anywhere suing the hospital for Cedric's death?"

Colin shook his head. "No, I heard they couldn't prove negligence on the part of the staff, so case closed."

On her way out to the parking lot, Marie got a call from Frankie who asked if Marie would accompany her to visit Faith in the women's prison. Marie was at a loss for words at first. It dawned on her that she was spending more time than ever before visiting people in prison. Finally, she said, "Uh, okay, but why do you want to do this?"

"Well, for the same reason you're knitting a baby blanket, Marie. This little one isn't even born yet, but he's already off to a bad start. If we can make up something of a village for him, why not do that?"

"How do you know it's a boy?" Marie smiled, and Frankie shrugged.

"Just a feeling. We can meet now before she has the baby, and give her time to get used to us."

Marie mulled it over. She'd originally thought she'd give the blanket to Colin to take to Faith as a gift without having any contact with that horrible woman, but maybe Frankie was right to want to establish a relationship of sorts for the child's sake.

"You don't think Colin will get back together with her someday, do you?" Frankie dared to ask.

"Good Lord, I hope not. He's made enough bad decisions already."

***

As she was choosing a cold drink at a convenience store near the hospital, Frankie felt a tap on her shoulder. When she turned, it took her a minute to process that she was looking at the bright, handsome face of Bryan Kennedy who she hadn't seen since Faith's trial. Frankie hadn't actually had a conversation with him, not even that time he stood up for her when Cedric said racist things in his hospital room. To Frankie, Bryan looked older, more mature than before even though the trial had ended just a while ago.

"Hey, how are you?" He asked with a shy smile.

"I'm pretty good. Bryan, is it?" When he nodded, she continued, "That was wild how you stepped up at the trial and said it was you who beat McCreary, then your dad's like 'No, it was me.'"

Bryan shook his head and glanced at the floor. "Yeah, I got shit for that."

"Hey, I never got a chance to thank you for sticking up for me that day."

The young man waved his hand to indicate that it had been no big deal. "My family knows a thing or two about racism. We've had beef with that old man's family for generations."

"Did you have to go to juvie?"

"Nah, I got off with community service, but I did go through a deradicalization program for something else." When he saw Frankie's eyes widen, Bryan was sorry he brought it up, but her face soon softened.

"Online stuff? That can really pull people in, or so I hear," she said sympathetically. They walked together up to the till, Frankie paid for her iced tea, and then they parted ways.

***

Faith woke up in a pool of liquid, puzzled at first. "Shit," she muttered, "my water broke. This baby is finally coming!" She called a guard over and was taken to the hospital to have her child. Colin, being incarcerated, wasn't allowed to attend the birth, but she didn't really want him there, anyway. She had never thought of him as someone she wanted to build a life with, and now that they were both in prison, well hell. Thankfully, the prison had cleared her mom to attend the birth.

Faith thought Colin had a strange relationship with Marie. How could you drunk drive into the back of a truck, killing your fiancee, and her mother still wants anything whatsoever to do with you? True, Marie seemed to be a super-nice person; she'd even come here with her friend Frankie to meet Faith, which was sweet since she didn't get many visitors except her own mom. The way they explained their interest was something about a village and a child. Whatever. Faith figured they could be useful to her too.

It was her first pregnancy and birth, long and painful. Fifteen hours of labour eventually produced a healthy baby boy of eight pounds, two ounces. Faith's mom held the baby shortly after it had gone for its initial check up, and then she placed him on Faith's chest, a bit reluctant to part with him.

Faith looked at the little guy and felt her heart soften.

"I feel something." She whispered to her mother. Faith had always felt that she was missing feelings that other people had, that something was very off about herself.

"He's a special one," her mother said in her heavily accented English. "Can you take a picture?" She said to the nurse, handing her camera to her.

The nurse took one with mother and child and then one of the three generations.

"Be sure to send a copy to Colin. Don't forget about him. He's the father," she scolded her daughter.

***

On her work break, Frankie put away her mop and bucket and washed her hands. She went down to the hospital cafeteria and bought herself a cup of coffee. As she sat down, she noticed Buddy across the room, also drinking coffee.

"Should I get his attention? Say hi?" She wondered. While she was pondering options, he noticed her and approached her table.

"Hi, Frankie. How are you?" She felt the awkwardness she always did when talking with men, but decided to look at his face instead of the table top for a change.

"I'm doing all right, Buddy. How about you?" She felt proud of herself for sounding like a normal person in these supposedly routine social interactions.

"Well, work's going well. I got promoted to detective after the McCreary case."

"Wow, that's great!" More quietly, she asked, "Is it weird not working with Colin anymore?" Then she wondered if that was too personal of a question.

Buddy did seem taken aback, but answered, "Yes, it is. I mean, we were friends and colleagues up to recently, but now he's in prison. It's very weird."

"I see Faith sometimes. Marie and I decided to reach out to her because the baby needs decent people growing up. Does that make sense, or are we messed up?"

Buddy raised his eyebrows. "It *is* unusual, I mean no one would blame you if you and especially Marie never wanted anything to do with her, the baby, or Colin again in your lives."

Frankie nodded. "I know. That was my first thought when I heard that it was Colin who hit the back of the truck and..." here her eyes welled up. She wiped at them with the sleeve of her uniform. "I was so angry at him, and then to find out he'd had an affair and that there's a baby..."

"Yeah, it's a lot."

"But he's been sober now for five months, so that's good. And anyway how else do we make this world less shitty?" Frankie asked. "I mean, I could hate Colin, hate Faith, and forget about their child, but what's that going to do? Maybe Faith wouldn't have been such a horrible person if she'd had more support. And Marie, well, she'd wanted to be a grandma long before Louise passed away. I mean, not that she's really the grandma, but you know."

"I know, but just be careful Faith doesn't use you, Frankie. You're a nice person and she's not. Be good to the child, but don't get sucked in and start giving Faith money or anything like that."

"I won't," Frankie agreed. "Hey, get this, she wanted to name the baby Darnell, if you can believe that, but Colin said no fucking way."

Buddy scoffed, "Of course not. Jesus. So what are they naming him?"

"Michael. Colin's dad's name and she went along with it. I guess she knows what side her bread is buttered on." Frankie pulled out her phone and found her most recent photo of Michael wrapped in the yellow blanket Marie had knitted. "Isn't he cute?"

Buddy smiled, and answered, "A real chip off the old block."

"I've been getting some counseling because of Louise's death, and for being charged with Cedric's beating." Frankie confided. "How has all of this affected *you*?"

Buddy fidgeted in his seat. "Well, there is someone available for cops to talk to, but I haven't checked it out. Mainly, I'm angry that Darnell died before we could bring him in. He should've been held accountable."

"At least Bubbles is doing some time for being an accessory after the fact though, right?"

Buddy nodded. "Yes, he's been given fourteen years, but may get out sooner."

"So what brings you to the hospital today, Buddy?"

"Oh, I just had some work business here," Buddy lied. The truth was he was driving by and decided to see if he could casually run into her, and somehow it had worked out. He said his goodbyes and left.

Frankie sipped her coffee while she Googled Indigenous events in her area. As a rule, she hadn't involved herself in much of the activities that were planned in her community, thinking she was too busy with work, or that there wasn't much point to it, but she'd changed over the last year. So much had happened, so many serious things in a short period of time, and she was different now. Frankie reflected on her time in the woods, and how it had a self-destructive feel to it. She'd set out naively thinking she knew more than she did about spending the night outdoors in the dead of winter. Her father was right. It had been reckless and dangerous.

Coming up was a weekend camp for Indigenous women focusing on outdoor life skills. This is great, thought Frankie. It covered a lot of what she could've used when she'd run away— foraging for safe foods in the woods, first aid, and food preparation in the backcountry. The price wasn't too bad. After a quick look at her bank balance, she decided to enroll. As she registered, she felt a quick thrill. It wasn't often she tried something new, preferring to stay with her comfortable routine. Immediately, she wondered if she should cancel her registration. Maybe this would be too hard or she'd get hypothermia again. "No," she thought, "stick with it. You can do this."

Chapter Twelve

August

William got a call from his mother that David wasn't doing so well;. His COPD was getting worse, and she didn't think he was getting enough oxygen even with his tank. William was still on house arrest, but Bryan got permission to drive them to the hospital to see his doctor.

Waiting for the elevator on her way back to her floor, Frankie ran into Bryan as he came out of it. He'd kept the afro although it was shorter than before, and he looked sporty in his track suit.

"Hey," he smiled shyly.

Geez, he's cute, Frankie thought again, smiling back. If only he was older. God, I'm turning into a creepy lady.

She asked, "What are you doing here? Is everything ok?"

"Well, my grandpa's not feeling well. I just dropped him off for a check up. I'm concerned about how he's doing."

"Oh, I'm sorry to hear that," she said sympathetically. "It's too bad I just finished my break or I'd have a coffee with you." Suddenly, Frankie was seized with the urge to ask him something she'd been noodling over for awhile.

"Hey, Bryan, that day you called Cedric out for being a dick to me, what did you whisper in his ear? It seemed to really rattle him."

Bryan chuckled self-consciously. "Oh, that. I told him that if he talked to you like that again I'd come back at night and beat the living shit out of him."

Frankie's jaw dropped. "You did?"

"Yes, and imagine his horror when someone, my freakin' dad actually, came in the night and actually did it. There's no *way* I could have predicted Dad'd do that. It didn't seem like who I always thought he was."

"Whew, it's like you and your dad were on the same wavelength."

"Yeah, I always thought we weren't, but yeah. We both got in a lot of trouble for all our shit though, so while we've kept our beliefs, we've taken the temperature down several notches."

"Well, that's good." Frankie waved goodbye and caught the next elevator up.

***

In the TV room at the women's prison, Faith sat in a sunbeam coming through the window, her son happily on her lap. It happened to be quiet and uncrowded that afternoon when she realized that Michael needed a diaper change. The television's sound was muted, so Faith didn't hear that the Royal Constabulary in Labrador City had located and charged a man suspected of Cedric McCreary's murder and indignity to a body. As she picked up her son and left the room, she didn't see the footage of a dead Darnell covered in a sheet on his way to the morgue.

Chapter Thirteen

Five Years Later

Bryan Kennedy was halfway through his university degree when David passed away. Although he deeply missed his grandpa, his father frequently reminded him that Grandad would be proud of him. He and William visited Ruth regularly. She'd moved into an assisted living facility after she lost her husband.

Due to good behaviour, no prior criminal record, and the child, Faith was released after only four years. She and Michael moved in with her mother who encouraged her to take the boy to see his father regularly, and she watched him while Faith worked at a nearby grocery store.

Colin had to serve at least seven years before he'd be eligible for release, but he'd earned enough money from his years of service to the Halifax Police Service to cover childcare support while in prison. In addition, he was taking advantage of the mechanics and auto repair programs to learn job skills for when he got out.

Marie Basque made the transition into a care home where she enjoyed the choir there as well as the knitting group. Faith, her mother, and Michael came to visit once a week. While she had never developed an affinity towards Faith, Marie loved Michael and his grandma who always arrived with homemade cookies to share. Michael, the spitting image of Colin, would be starting kindergarten in the fall. The very fact of this bright little boy's existence seemed a sort of miracle to Marie.

With the help of a social worker, Frankie was able to contact her mother, something she'd always wanted to do but had been afraid of rejection. The social worker encouraged her to go for it and she learned that her mother had been living in Eskasoni, a First Nations community near Bras d'Or Lake. Kiknu was a residential home with 48 private suites and sounded pretty decent. After the social worker brokered a meeting with Frankie's "giju" (the Mikmaq word for mother which sounds like gee-choo), Frankie drove over three hours northeast to see her for the first time since she was a girl.

She pulled into the visitor parking at a modern low-story building with views of the lake.

"Wow," Frankie thought as she paused to take in the sky, water, and the beautifully landscaped grounds which featured a full-size teepee. She took a moment to take a deep breath and then entered a spacious foyer with floor to ceiling windows and wooden support beams. The feel was contemporary with traditional First Nations features.

In the sitting area in an armchair, sat Giju wrapped in a Pendleton blanket. Since Frankie had never had much opportunity to interact with her, she didn't know how to address her. She decided to just ask.

"Hello," she said softly as she sat down in a nearby chair. The petite woman in the chair tried to get up but seemed too frail, so Frankie gestured for her to remain seated.

"What should I call you?"

Her mother's rheumy eyes welled up, and she didn't answer right away.

"Giju?" Frankie asked gently.

Her mother smiled and nodded, wiping her nose with a tissue.

"It's good to see you, Frankie."

"It's so good to see you, too."

"I've missed you," Giju sobbed quietly. "I'm sorry I left. I had to leave your father, and I didn't think I could raise you." She pulled a Kleenex out of the box on the coffee table.

Frankie reached over and touched her mother on the shoulder. Just like she hadn't been sure how to address her, she also wasn't sure how much touch was okay.

"It was hard sometimes, mom. Really hard." She decided to be honest.

Giju nodded furiously while blowing her nose. "I know. I know you went to foster care."

"Yeah, I was lucky though. At least I got a good one."

"I'm so glad for that. The social worker told me about your troubles with your friend Louise and the murder."

"Those were some troubles, all right," Frankie chuckled. "I'm doing okay now."

"Do you have a husband or kids?" Giju asked.

Frankie shook her head. "I dated a nice guy for a while, Buddy, but in the end we were just too different. He was a cop."

"Oh," Giju said, raising her eyebrows.

"I know, right? After the initial attraction, we just didn't really understand where the other was coming from, if you know what I mean." Frankie was surprised how much she was telling her mother. Maybe she had a pent-up need to share with her, was trying to make up for lost time.

"Well, I've dated a few white guys in my time, so yeah, I think I do." Giju smiled.

Frankie's face lit up. "I don't have kids of my own, but there's a boy who calls me "Aunty"— Colin's son." She explained Michael's family situation as best she could.

"The social worker said you worked at a hospital. Are you still there?"

"Yes, but I've been looking around for something different. I worked for a kids' camp as a counselor last summer, so maybe I could get on full-time with the organization that runs it."

Eventually, Giju stifled a yawn and Frankie took that as her cue to wrap things up. She stood up and said, "Can I give you a hug?"

"I thought you'd never ask," Giju answered, eyes glistening. They shared a long embrace where Frankie closed her eyes and allowed herself to relax into it.

She assured her mother that she'd be in touch and would come to visit again. On her way past the reception desk, a bulletin board with notices caught Frankie's eye. As it turned out, the Kiknu residential home had several job positions open. Frankie took photos of the job descriptions and contact information to examine in more detail later.

As she sat in her car, she imagined a different life from the one she'd had in Halifax, one with more nature and regular contact with her mother. Something caught her eye above, and she looked up to see a bald eagle flying overhead. Once it was out of sight, she turned her music on, put on sunglasses, cracked a cold can of Coke that she'd bought inside, and drove back to Halifax.

★★★★★★★★★★★★